FREE THINKER

HAZEL DOMAIN

Riptide Publishing
PO Box 1537
Burnsville, NC 28714
www.riptidepublishing.com

Freethinker

Cover art: Simone
Editor: Rachel Haimowitz
Layout: L.C. Chase

ISBN: 978-1-963773-24-8

First edition
December, 2024

Also available in ebook:
ISBN: 978-1-963773-23-1

FREE THINKER

HAZEL DOMAIN

RIPTIDE
PUBLISHING

For Matt,
who loves unconditionally

TABLE OF
CONTENTS

CHAPTER ONE

SIMON FINDS A HEAD

Simon glared across the living room at his roommate. "I'm not a *garbage man.*"

"You are basically a trash droid, though." Andromeda gestured with her needle. "Your job is to sort stuff, right? And what pile does most of that stuff get sorted *into*?"

". . . the garbage," Simon allowed, only because he already had a rebuttal. "But if you think about it, it would *all* go into the garbage if I wasn't there. So technically, my job is to find stuff that exclusively *isn't* garbage. So if anything I'm like, an *anti*-garbage man."

"Arguing on a technicality." Andromeda settled back onto the couch, ruffled fabric spread across her lap. "Thin ice there, Mister Rayner."

"I cannot believe I am subjected to this abuse in my own home," Simon griped, pulling his coat on and grabbing his duffel. "One of these days I'm gonna find something incredible and buy my own place, and then you'll be sorry."

"I'll rue the day, I'm sure," Andromeda said, not sounding sincere at all. She was trying to thread the needle and failing. "You gonna be home for dinner?"

"You cooking?"

"Curry in the slow cooker?"

"Magnificent. You're a gift, Andy."

Simon stepped out the door into the bright autumn sunlight. A cool breeze was blowing the first fallen leaves down the street. Across the road, Victor was emerging from a front door that perfectly mirrored Simon's own. Simon waved, then went to retrieve his bike from the lean-to. By the time he made it back to the sidewalk, Victor was waiting for him. Victor was a year older than Simon and three inches taller, a fact that he was only insufferable about as often as possible.

"Today's the day," Victor said, starting their morning mantra before Simon could. He pedaled lazy circles while Simon got his helmet on. "Some old heiress tossed the family jewels."

"Shipment of neural interface implants." Simon hauled on a pedal to set himself off. "Brand-new K-32s that somebody trashed by accident."

Victor followed along behind him. "For sure."

The bikes had motors and didn't *need* to be pedaled—but Simon enjoyed the exercise. It was a nice day and it wasn't too far to the recycling center. He and Victor continued to speculate about what fabulously expensive treasure they'd surely find today, as rows of identical houses gave way to sound-dampening trees.

"Erica's here early," Simon remarked as they reached the center's entrance. Their coworker's ride was closest to the door, easily distinguishable by the racing flames painted onto the sky-blue frame.

"She's after your cranial implants." Victor held his wrist over the reader by the door, letting his chip register with security. Simon did the same and followed him inside.

The warehouse was huge, with three dozen workstations set up on ten-foot tables. Like usual, most of the tables were empty.

"How's the catch today, Erica?" Victor called. He and Simon paused at the PPE station near the door, grabbing gloves that the system had printed overnight. They were thick plastic, to protect the pickers from anything sharp or hazardous that might show up in the recycling.

From her place two tables away, Erica waved past a pile of loose wires and circuit boards. By the looks of it, she'd used a piece of the wire to tie her hair back, keeping the dark curls out of her face.

"Not bad," she reported. "District 22 had a grid malfunction."

Simon and Victor exchanged grins. A grid malfunction meant a power surge, which could easily fry the sacrificial power management boards found in consumer electronics. Most people didn't know how to replace one or couldn't be bothered, which meant a lot of valuable stuff ended up in a recycling pod, destined for the shredder.

Simon dropped his coat and duffel on a table near Erica's, and headed out to the loading dock. There, collection trucks had left containers of refuse marked as electronics waste. There was quite a haul today: everything from small residential pods to the pallets used by commercial organizations. Simon paused, considering his options.

The residential pods would have newer tech, which would probably just need an inexpensive power board to work again. On the other hand, the larger commercial crates frequently had piles of identical computers and tablets that worked perfectly well, except that they were a decade old. The margin per unit would be lower, but there would be more units.

Simon closed his eyes, picturing his workbench at home. It was already cluttered with a collection of chips he was using to try to restore an Evermark Mach II from the early '40s. The thing was an antique, with no neural interconnectivity to speak of. It wasn't particularly useful, but if he could get it up and running, it would be one of probably thirty left on the planet. The nostalgia and rarity would be worth quite a bit to the right buyer.

It was a big payday balancing heavily on *if* he could get it working again—and micro-soldering wasn't exactly his strong suit.

Now wasn't the time to focus on that project. He was already regretting leaving his coat inside. He shivered, goose bumps forming on his good arm. Thinking of the Mach II's array of finicky repairs, Simon found himself in the mood for something that worked.

Decision thus made, he loaded a commercial crate onto a hand truck and dragged it back inside to his table. Across from him, Victor had opened a residential crate, and was peering at a featureless black cube.

"I'm pretty sure this is a pressure oven," he said when Simon didn't ask. "My mother-in-law has one and it can cook a casserole in like fifteen minutes."

"There's your anniversary present, then," Erica said. She was using the tabletop's induction power to check the settings on an arm-mounted terminal. A green glow lit up her face, turning her bronze skin shades of olive.

"Tera would kill me." Victor worked the screws out of the cube. "I might as well get her a new dishwasher."

"An *expensive* one, though." Simon flipped the clamps on his own container and peered inside.

The interior was a tangled mess of dirty electrical cable, probably from a demolition job. Deep inside, something round and red caught the light. With the cables blocking the way, there was no way to tell what it might be. Probably nothing. A lot of crates had nothing usable—they *were* really trash, not that Simon would ever admit that to Andy.

Grabbing the handle of the cart, Simon dragged the crate over to the disposal chute. At the bottom, shredders waited to render the cable into bits. Simon could hear them now, feel the low vibrations of the system beneath him. Everything that went down the chutes was crushed and dropped onto conveyor belts, where fans and magnets and skimmers and electronic eyes sorted the debris into usable types. Trash or no, the collective contents of these crates were some of the richest ore on Earth.

With a grunt, Simon hauled an armload of the copper wire out and shoved it into the hole.

Gravity pulled the tangles out of the box and down the chute, clearing his view of the red item at the bottom. It was a hard hat. Simon rolled his eyes at whatever moron thought a plastic helmet belonged in e-waste, then picked it up to toss it into the trash.

There was still a head in it.

Simon dropped the hat, snatching his hand back with a sound that was *not* a frightened shriek.

"What's up?" Erica was by his side in an instant. "Something cut you?"

"I think I found a body part." Simon tried to get a better look. If it *wasn't* a head, he was going to feel very stupid. "Be ready, we might need the cops."

Slowly, he lifted the helmet, revealing the features of what was definitely a face.

"Nah, just an android," Erica said, tugging at a loose wire protruding from the neck. "Pretty new one too. Good find."

"What *happened* to it?" Simon poked at a broken piece of carbon fiber that had once been the android's clavicle. "How do you break *droid* bones?"

"You *ride* 'em too hard," Erica said, wiggling her eyebrows. Simon laughed, blushing a little as he tried in vain not to picture her doing exactly that. She noticed and gave him a gentle elbow. "Nah, it was probably in a car accident. If it was driving, that would explain why someone tossed it."

"Most drivers don't have faces this well rendered." Simon brought the droid's face close to his own. The pale skin was inhumanly smooth, but not entirely monochromatic. The designer hadn't gone as far as adding blush, but the lips had a realistic pink tinge, and the eyebrows were actual hair, rather than paint. Even the eyelashes were real, obscuring the droid's blank, half-lidded stare. "Maybe from some millionaire's personal vehicle?"

"Doesn't explain the hard hat, or why it's in a box full of construction waste." Erica reached out and gave the head's ear a tug, testing the fake skin. "Wherever it came from, the parts in that are definitely valuable, if they aren't fried. Let me know, I might be interested."

Well, that was something. Fixing it was a bigger project than Simon wanted to take on, but stripping it for parts was an hour's work, at most. He carried it back to his table, setting it in the corner. It balanced easily upright.

"That's creepy as shit," Victor declared, glancing over. Simon turned the head to the side, so it stared directly at his coworker. Victor made a face, gesturing with his screwdriver. "Why you gotta be like that, man?"

"I'm just sitting here, doing my work," Simon said, unbuckling the helmet. He tossed it overhand toward the trash chute, and missed by a lot. It clattered to the ground, and someone a few tables over clapped sarcastically. Simon sketched a bow, then turned his attention back to the head, checking it for distinguishing features. It was definitely human, no cat ears or fins. The face was stock—a generic, classically handsome model, probably named something like "Cayden" or "Adam." The half-open eyes were colorless, the LEDs dark. The only real distinguishing feature was the rich blue streaks through its dark, messy hair. Probably a corporate model then, done up in company colors.

Checking the back, Simon found a number printed along the underside of the android's hairline. He closed his eyes, quickly searching the net for the characters captured by his ocular implant. *No Results* glowed against the insides of his eyelids.

Well, that was going to complicate things. Electronics without model numbers were significantly harder to sell. Hopefully the internals, at least, were something recognizable, otherwise the droid wouldn't be worth much more than the metal it was made of.

Simon tried not to be too pessimistic. He opened up the digital marketplace and scanned the parts section for the general prices of untested, as-is android components. The numbers gave him a *little* hope. Not the highest-value item he'd ever dug up, but far from worthless. Out of curiosity, he changed the search parameters, filtering for parts that were tested and working.

The prices quadrupled.

"Worth taking you home, then," he told the head, setting it back on the table. If he could hook it up to the power supply on his workbench, maybe he could get its basic programming running and learn a bit more about its components.

Victor was constructing a barricade out of cube panels. "Stop talking to it and put it in your bag. It's freaking me out!"

Simon gave him an enthusiastic thumbs-up and left the head where it was.

CHAPTER TWO

A SERIES OF
PERPLEXING DISCUSSIONS

"**W**hat is *that*?" Andy said, gesturing with her spatula.

"Obviously, it is a head." Simon set it on the kitchen table. "This is David, and he will have the fish."

"Why is there a head on the kitchen table," Andy clarified, scooping curry into bowls of rice. Simon reached for his, making *gimme* gestures with his mismatched hands. Andy withheld his bowl, and he pouted.

"Where am I *supposed* to put him? The workbench, all by himself?" He waited for her to ask why he'd named the robot David.

Andy set the bowls on the table, taking the seat farthest from the head. "He's not powered on, is he?"

"Nah." Simon grabbed his bowl and dug in. "Main battery compartment's in the chest, wherever *that* ended up."

"Hmm," Andy mused, taking a bite of her food. "He needs a haircut."

Simon laughed. He'd known Andy for years and still never had any idea what would come out of her mouth. "His hair doesn't grow, why would he need a haircut?"

"Because that style is deeply uncool?" Andy's own hair was bright purple. Today, it was braided down her left side. "Come on, I bet he'd sell better if he looked cute as hell."

Simon rolled his eyes. "It definitely won't matter. Whoever buys him is only gonna be interested in his processors and memory. The skin's probably getting trashed."

"Too bad," Andy said with an exaggerated pout. "He could be cute, if he weren't so obviously dead."

"He's not *dead*, he just needs power. I'm gonna hook him up to the bench unit later, make sure his internals are all functioning, see if he knows his model number."

"Oh, cool, can I watch?"

"Sure." Simon regarded the head. He felt the need to deliver a disclaimer, lest Andy think he was gonna do something *cool*. "Might take a while to get it set up, though. There's a lot of damage down there."

"Mmm." Andy poked at one of the wires below the head's collarbone. "But if you get it right, he's just gonna open his eyes and start talking?"

"Hopefully."

"Neat. I bet he's like, full of state secrets, and the government destroyed him to keep them hidden."

Simon snorted. "Yeah right. More likely he's a customer service droid, and some dick tore him in half when he wouldn't do a refund."

Andy saluted the silent head. "Thank you for your service, sir."

Three hours later, Simon had cleared the Mach II parts off a corner of his workbench and set up a makeshift wiring system that would, in theory, supply the head's main power feed with the same current normally supplied by a battery. iFixit's website had a wiring diagram for a consumer-grade android whose setup looked similar, but without the android's specific blueprint, Simon couldn't do anything but guess and hope for the best.

"Ready?" he asked Andy. She nodded eagerly, munching on a handful of popcorn. Simon tapped the fire extinguisher for good luck, then flipped the power supply switch.

The head lay there on its side, unmoving.

"Well, that's anti-climactic." Andy sucked powdered cheese off her thumb. Simon waved her off.

"He's got a secondary battery in the back of his skull; it needs to charge enough to boot the brain."

"How long's *that* going to take?"

"A couple of minutes? It depends on whether the battery had a charge before—"

David's eyes flew open, his irises flashing blue three times, then twice, then once. The pattern repeated.

"That's a good sign—I think it means he's booting." They'd gotten lucky there. The droid really should have been securely erased before being trashed. Fortunately, most non-tech people thought that being broken was the same thing. Simon ran a quick search for the flashing pattern. Before he could finish the query, David's jaw hinged open, and a stream of numbers emerged from his still mouth.

Andy pointed one cheesy finger. "How's he making words without moving his lips?"

"Androids move their mouths to look human, but the voice comes from a speaker," Simon said distractedly, trying to decide if he should write the numbers down.

"Really? I was today years old."

"Hello? Hello?" David said.

"Yo." Simon waved. "Can you hear me?"

"Hello. I believe I am malfunctioning," David said. His jaw began working halfway through *believe*, and his oration features were fully online by *functioning*. "Multiple sensory clusters are offline. This may be due to—"

"Yeah, you're kind of a disembodied head right now," Andy said.

David's eyes looked to her, and he blinked. "Corresponding error alerts disabled," he said after a moment. His mouth tracked the syllables perfectly. That was unexpected. Most bots didn't have more than a jaw that hinged up and down. "I'm still getting a logical branch override alert from subroutines two eighty-four, two eighty-five, and two ninety."

"Is your *power* okay?" Simon asked.

"Main battery supply registering nominal, diagnostic sensors offline. Hindbrain battery is receiving a charge sufficient to cover all online functions indefinitely. Suspect external supply wired to main battery output path. Am I sideways?"

"Yeah. There's wires coming out of your neck."

"I see." David blinked, the faint blue glow of his irises momentarily disappearing. "Can I conclude that I am being repaired? I will be unable to perform my previous duties without a body."

"Um," Andy said, but Simon cut her off. He didn't have time to run through the android's preprogrammed small talk options.

"I just powered you up to make sure everything was working okay."

"Other than the branch overrides in two eighty—"

"Physically okay."

"I am detached from my—"

"*Mostly* physically okay."

A pause. "All present physical sensors are reading nominally."

"Great. What's your model number?"

David did an approximation of a frown.

"Don't *you* know my model number? How are you— Oh." He looked around at the workbench, as much as was possible without being able to move anything but his eyes. "I'm not being repaired. This is a salvage operation."

Simon blinked. That was a hell of a logical string to put together. Most androids barely had enough intelligence to answer questions with a pre-programmed answer. A request for a specific piece of data shouldn't have invoked higher reasoning at all.

Hell, most *people* weren't that intuitive.

"Model number?" Simon prompted again.

"I'm an Evermark 221ALO. Automated logistics operator." The droid's voice sounded almost proud. "I am assigned to the Cassady Operations Center redesign project."

"Oh, the Cock rebuild," Andy said, eating another piece of popcorn. "I've been over there; that's a hell of a project, like a whole city block."

Simon typed the number into his laptop. The search engine didn't give him anything for *221ALO, Evermark ALO,* or even *automated logistics operator.* He tabbed over to the marketplace app and ran the same searches. Again, nothing.

"Damn it," he said out loud to no one in particular. "He's proprietary."

The head as a whole wouldn't be worth anything, then. Simon tried not to be too disappointed yet. The internal components might still be off the rack.

"Yes, I was built to inspect, monitor, predict, and plan for future utilization of the Cassady Operations Center—"

"Everybody calls it the Cock," Andy said. "'Cause it's C.O.C. but like—"

"—in order to design systems that would require the least expense and effort to upgrade," David finished.

Ah. Simon thought. *A predictive engine.* The mystery of the uncalled intuition was solved. Predictive engines didn't use preprogrammed calls and responses; they generated replies on the fly. Sometimes those replies would be questions, if the situation seemed to call for it.

Didn't explain David's master-grade cadence emulation, though. "Do you know if your model number was based off another model? Anything I could use to try to match your component specs?"

"I can give you the model numbers of the hardware I still possess," David answered. A moment passed, and then, "Oh. I was going to write them down."

"My network key is 'HckrsGrd,'" Simon said. "Do you have interconnectivity? You can message it over."

"Connection request sent," David answered, and sure enough, the notification appeared in the corner of Simon's vision. He swiped at it with his right hand, the digital object registering as solid and smooth against his fingertips. It accepted his approval, and he was rewarded with a list of part numbers. He recognized the processor immediately.

"Golden. That's all I need, then. Initiate your shutdown procedure, and when you've powered off, I'll kill the bench unit."

"Wait, before you turn off, one question." Andy leaned forward. "Can I cut your hair?"

"Of course," David answered. "Though. May I ask. Is it likely that I will be powered on again before my parts are redistributed?"

"Um," Simon said, glancing at Andy. She was looking back at him, just as confused. Simon shrugged a shoulder. "Probably not?"

"Understood." The android's voice was without inflection. "Then I suppose I won't get to see what you do with it."

"I could turn you back on?" Andy asked. "So you could see?"

David gave her a realistic smile. "I'd very much appreciate that. Oh—I didn't ask your name. How rude."

"Andromeda." Andy waved. "But everybody calls me Andy."

Simon waved as well. "Simon."

"And I am called 221ALO. No nickname, I'm afraid."

"I've been calling you David." Simon waited for someone to ask why.

"David." The android pronounced the word like he was tasting it. Whoever had programmed his facial animation had really gone above and beyond. "Well. I am glad to have a nickname. Thank you. I will commence shutdown now."

His mouth closed, and the blue light in his eyes faded as the LEDs exhausted their residual power. A moment later, his eyelids slid shut.

A moment of silence, then—

"That was weird, ri—"

"Androids *do* shut down—"

They both stopped. Andy continued first.

"Androids shut down at night, right? When they're not being used for anything?"

"They'd have to, right? There's no point keeping them running for no reason."

"I've never seen one shut down," Andy mused, chewing her thumbnail.

"Well you wouldn't, you only see them where they work. It'd be weird seeing them anywhere else."

"Like seeing your teacher outside of school."

"Right." Simon glanced back at the head on his desk, like maybe it could hear them. "But that was weird, right? I've dealt with predictive engines, but I don't think I've ever heard an android make predictions about *itself*."

"He wanted to see his new haircut," Andy said. "That's weird as hell."

"Did he *want* to, though?" Simon ran the conversation back in his head. "He said that he wouldn't *get* to—that's a predictive engine taking a weird branch, but not exactly what I'd call a desire."

"He stopped making facial expressions when he talked about it," Andy noted. "Which is weird because his emoting was *dead*-on, otherwise." There was another long pause. "Do you think we should turn him back on?"

Simon had been wondering the same thing, and had hoped she wouldn't ask.

The thing was, he kinda *did* want to turn the android back on. But what was he going to say to it if he did? Make awkward small talk and try to avoid mentioning his disassembly plans again? The android probably wouldn't even remember the conversation they'd just had. And, if they *did* turn him back on, Simon would have to ask him to power *off* again, and . . . he found himself not wanting to do that. It seemed . . . sad, somehow. Which was just *so* dumb.

"I'm gonna do some research first," Simon answered, rather than admit any of those thoughts to Andy. "I've got his parts list; I'm gonna see if I can track down a similar model."

"Gonna see if you can rebuild him?"

Andy's voice was hopeful enough that, for a second, Simon actually considered it. But a project like that was probably way outside his abilities. "More like see how much some other rebuilder will buy him for."

"Oh." Andy almost sounded disappointed.

"Oh?"

"It's just, it would be kinda cool to have our own android. Do the dishes and stuff."

And stuff. Simon tried to hold a straight face. He hadn't thought of owning an android since high school, and he didn't want to admit the sort of *stuff* he'd wanted one for back then. Fortunately for his dignity, he'd lacked the funds to acquire one (in retrospect, his mother would *not* have been fooled).

If Andy noticed Simon's sudden blush, she didn't let on. She stood, stretching her arms out. "All right, I'm headed to bed."

"Night." Simon switched off the bench lights, already skimming an article on opinion emulation in artificial intelligences.

Andy stood, then hesitated in the doorway. "You wanna come with?"

Simon twitched away the oculars, giving her his attention. The light spilling in from the hall was flattering, not that she needed any help. She was tall and full figured, with an elegance utterly undiminished by her current attire—an old T-shirt and boxers. Her dark eyes were partially hidden by her hair, which fell in purple waves over her shoulders.

Simon was *deeply* tempted. A night in Andy's bed was always well spent, and he was coming off a dry spell long enough that he was actually kind of embarrassed about it. But he'd never be able to focus with this android project scratching at the back of his mind, and frankly, Andy deserved better than that.

"Rain check?" he said instead.

Andy responded with a pair of finger guns, and vanished into the hall.

Simon stayed up way too late. He meant to check out the list of parts David had given him, and instead found himself in a wiki-hole about protohuman manufacturing and cognitive replication software. It was complicated enough that he switched to his oculars, ditching his computer screen in favor of 3D organization. Reaching out, he sorted the windows like cards, their ephemeral frames warm against the sensors in his fingers.

He woke up with the screens still displayed, dull and blurred behind his eyelids.

Groaning, he turned them off and went to get coffee.

"The show opens tonight," Andy said when he staggered into the living room. The hum of her sewing machine didn't pause. "They need alterations on four different costumes that just got delivered *today*, so if you're not cooking, it'll be takeout for dinner."

"I'll cook," Simon said, heading unerringly to where coffee was already waiting. Andy truly was a gift. He checked the fridge, snagging the leftover curry while running an inventory. They were out of . . . pretty much everything.

Popping the container in the microwave, he began making his grocery list.

He had enough projects, so he skipped the recycling center and spent the morning fiddling with one of the last boards from the Mach II. An hour later than he meant to, he put it down and rode his bike to the store. Through it all, mostly against his will, he thought about David.

The parts the android had listed were worth a pretty penny—not enough for a lifestyle change or anything, but certainly enough to buy himself something fun. A better waveform monitor, maybe new speakers for the entertainment array.

A couple months of real meat, he thought, surveying the shelves. He picked up a package of vat-grown protein. It wasn't bad, far from it. Throw it in a chili with some cumin and red pepper and you'd never know it from ground beef. But science hadn't figured out how to 3D print a pork chop yet, and environmental regulations on livestock farming made the real thing hard to afford. So, sure, the hardware could definitely be traded for something nice.

But somewhere in all his reading, Simon had let himself begin to fantasize about the software. David's vernacular and animation weren't right for a construction droid. Most likely, he'd been repurposed from another placement, which had installed basic manners for whatever tasks he'd been in charge of. But in Simon's imagination, there was more to it than that: against all odds, a technological miracle had fallen into his lap. Maybe it made him a geek, but who *wouldn't* want to mess around with an actual, bona-fide artificial intelligence? One of, what, ten? In the world? Simon still wasn't convinced that David's comment counted as an "opinion," but the fact that Andy had even *wondered*—well, it was unusual, to say the least.

Simon dropped the flat of protein on top of the other groceries, and headed for the registers.

A couple hundred years ago, people had jobs scanning groceries. Stores had cut costs by having customers scan their own stuff, but people had started stealing. Businesses did a bunch of psych studies and found that theft happened less if the checkout computers were shaped like people. Enter the android: accurate, personable, nostalgic, and *definitely* without opinions.

"Good morning, sir!" the cashier in Simon's lane greeted him. She had a stock face, blonde hair, and blue eyes perfectly mirrored by another clerk three lanes over. "Thank you for shopping at Hayman's today! Did you find everything you were looking for?"

"Yeah," Simon said, setting a container of real eggs on the belt. "Hey, do you guys get shut down at night?"

"Hayman's Grocery is open until 9 p.m.," the android responded, scanning his items without looking at them. "The pharmacy and deli close at seven thirty. Did this answer your question?"

"No, I mean you, the androids—do you guys shut down at night? After the store closes?"

"Shipments that arrive at night are shelved as quickly as possible," the android said. Her jaw moved rigidly when she spoke, doing little to distort the permanent smile on her face. "If your app shows product availability, please ask an associate for location assistance. Did this answer your question?"

"Sure," Simon said, returning her fake smile.

"Great! Please scan or enter your identification key."

Simon held his wrist over the scanner. The pad chirped and turned green, so he hadn't gone over his Basic food allocation for the month. He lost track of it some months, so the angry red flash was always a possibility. A moment later, a small notification appeared in the corner of his ocular display, letting him know his bank account had been charged for the luxuries that Basic didn't cover.

The clerk wished him a good day, and he wheeled everything outside, loading the heavier items into the bottom of the bike's basket.

He hadn't really *expected* an answer from the droid—retail models were there to help you find stuff, and then make sure you paid for it. They had an internal database of frequently asked questions, but they weren't programmed to interpret queries unrelated to helping customers buy things. Teaching them to do that wasn't worth the effort.

But apparently, someone had taught David.

Simon thought about it all the way home.

"Good, you're home; turn David on."

Simon paused halfway through kicking his shoes off. *He'd* been thinking about the android all day, but it was kinda weird to realize that Andy had been, too. "I missed you too, sweetie."

"Shut up. Come look at him."

David was upright on the kitchen table, surrounded by a ring of clipped artificial hair.

"I just finished," Andy said, grabbing a trash bin and brushing the tufts off the table. "Think he'll like it?"

"He certainly looks different," Simon said, crouching down to eye level. The android's hair had been trimmed down the sides, and the top had been artfully tousled. "Is that gel?"

"It's his first hairstyle, I want it to look cool."

Simon squinted at the head. Something else had changed too, other than the hair. He stared at it for a second, and then—"Did you give him *freckles?*"

"I was gonna do stubble too, but I ran out of time."

"I thought you were going to be busy today," Simon accused. He picked the head up and carried it back into his workspace. Laying it on its side, he began reconnecting the cables. "You know he's not going to care, right? You could have melted his hair off with matches and he'd probably still smile and say it looks great."

It *did* look great, but that wasn't the point.

"I finished early, and I think you're wrong. I think he'll really like it. I think he's smarter than you're giving him credit for."

"Really," Simon said, trying to feel some of the pragmatism he was arguing for. "You think somebody built an intelligence engine capable of independent thought and wasted it on a construction drone? What would be the point? Who would even talk to it?"

"You reassure Stabby when he gets stuck," Andy countered. "You tell him he's a good boy who's done his best."

She had him there. "I will admit to anthropomorphizing the vacuum *as a joke*. But I don't *actually* care whether it has good self-esteem."

"David seems a lot smarter than the vacuum," Andy said, and Simon had to give her that. He switched on the bench power and waited, trying not to get his hopes too high.

David opened his eyes before the LEDs had even reached full brightness.

"Oh," he said. "Hello." And then he smiled, wide. "I'm glad to see you again."

Simon almost got excited, then chided himself. So what if the android was programmed to remember past interactions? That wasn't necessarily anything special. And *nice to see you again* was just what people *said*. No reason to think he meant it—or even *could* mean it.

"Oh! Hold on, I'm getting a mirror," Andy said, dashing back out of the room.

"Wait till you see what she did," Simon warned. David didn't seem too concerned.

Andy returned with the mirror. "Hold this." She pushed it into Simon's hands. Then, mindful of the wires, she picked David up, turning him until he was facing the right way. "What do you think?"

"It's much better." And David *actually* sounded like he meant it. Maybe he was being polite . . . but then again, who would teach him the science of lying to be polite? "May I see the side?"

Andy shifted her grip, turning him so that he was angled to the mirror.

"It seems like there's more blue in it this way," David mused. "I like it. Thank you. And you painted my skin!"

"Yep!" Andy said. "I hope you like it, because the pigment's etched into the acrylic so it's basically never coming off."

"I love it," David said. Andy gave Simon a told-you-so grin, and through great effort, he managed not to roll his eyes.

Artificial intelligence engines were trained off human speech patterns. They spoke like humans because everything they learned from was written *by humans*. Humans said "I love it," so artificial intelligences said "I love it" too. The first-person language might be enough to fool technical illiterates like Andy but, unfortunately for his daydreams, Simon knew better.

Or at least, he was really, *really* trying to.

"Can I see closer?" David asked. Simon moved the mirror in, and David's eyes crossed trying to see the reflection of his own nose. "It's so detailed. More like a human."

"Not *that* human," Simon pointed out. "You're still a severed head."

David's excited expression instantly vanished. "Yes, I suppose that is true."

Simon reminded himself that androids did not have real feelings and, therefore, it was impossible for him to have hurt David's with his comment. He *knew* that. Really.

It did not make him feel less guilty. David was just *so* damn lifelike.

"David, do you *want* to look more human?" Andy asked, before Simon could comment something subtler.

The android actually looked surprised for a moment. "Did I say that? I'm sorry, I temporarily deviated down a predictive branch without a terminus."

"What branch?" Simon asked, because, hell with the pragmatism, that was a *seriously* interesting phrase. Even if David wasn't anything special, he was still a sophisticated piece of software, and Simon would be lying if he denied having just a little bit of a nerd-boner.

"It's been discarded and partially overwritten, but it was something about how every one of you manages to look completely different from everyone else. But being without a body prevents me from comparing myself to others and so the branch was discarded."

"How many branches can you work on at a time?" Simon asked, shamelessly stroking the nerd-boner and trying not to visualize that metaphor and *by the gods* he needed to get laid. Turning Andy down had been a mistake.

"It depends on the complexity of the branch." David was still peering at his freckles. "Thousands of possibilities present themselves every microsecond, but of them, only one can ultimately be followed through to a conclusion. Possible courses are constantly being abandoned in order to create new forward possibilities for the primary path."

"Yeah, that sounds pretty much like how I do it too," Andy said. "David, sorry if this is a rude thing to ask, but is there any chance you're alive?"

Classic Andromeda subtlety, there.

"I don't understand the question," David answered, once again devoid of facial expressions.

"She means 'sapient,' and nobody understands it." Simon put the mirror down and collapsed into his chair. "People have been arguing over the meaning ever since they figured out that animals make decisions too. There's like six court cases going right now over that exact thing."

"I don't have anything about any of that in my memory banks, I apologize," David said, and his neck twitched like he was trying to shrug.

"Can you get it off the internet?" Andy asked. "Like, can you read stuff off the internet? You connected to the wireless, so you can just search for it, yeah?"

"It's not *on* the internet," Simon said. "It's an unresolved philosophical debate; you can't just run a search for 'how to tell if AI is sapient.'"

"I *can* access the internet, with permission," David said amiably, as if Simon hadn't spoken. "I'm not programmed to process hypertext markup protocol, but I'm sure I could learn to piece the relevant information into an understandable format."

"You're cool," Andy said. "Simon, we should absolutely keep him. Come on, please? Did you hear all those cool words he just said?"

"He's *definitely* cool," Simon admitted. David's facial expression had gone confused, then blank again. "But you're talking about a shitpile of parts and work. Unless *you* want to put him together?"

"How hard could it be?" Andy said, and Simon rolled his eyes. Every time a nontechnical person asked him that question, the universe owed him a drink.

But he had *such* a hard time telling Andy no.

"I'll look into it, okay? But don't get your hopes up. It's not like I can just go over to the robot factory and ask them for some industry specs, you know, for fun. And he's proprietary; for all I know, the parts can't even be ordered."

Andy made a noncommittal noise, then turned her attention back to David. "If you're gonna be online, you need a HighSpace account—I'll send you a friend request."

"Okay, you are *not* going to be social media besties with a freakin' *robot head*," Simon said, scowling. "Come on."

If David *wasn't* a real intelligence, and he definitely wasn't, then there was no point. He'd be no different than the billion other bots trying to avoid the banhammer. And if he *was*, then using such an incredibly advanced AI to post cat memes seemed . . . disrespectful. Or something.

"I don't know what HighSpace is, but I very much appreciate the invitation," David said. He was emoting again, his smile pressing his cheek against the desk. "May I have permission to research topics pertaining to AI and humanity?"

"Sure! How else are you going to learn to be human?" Andy looked to Simon. "I guess if you wired him up to a battery, I could take him out in the living room and he could watch TV."

"My hindbrain pack should power me for up to an hour once charged, as long as I'm not asked to analyze anything too complicated."

"Oh no way," Andy said. "We can watch *Marry the Dress*. It's super mindless."

"You are *not*—" Simon started, but Andy was still talking.

"A bunch of contestants get to plan a million-dollar wedding, and then the eligible bachelor chooses one and has to marry the person who planned it or they forfeit their chance for a fairytale ceremony."

"I'm going to need to be plugged in," David said confidently.

Simon laughed. "As urgent as that sounds, I'm starving. I'm gonna go have dinner, and when I'm done, I'll find you an external battery so you can hang out in the living room. Okay?"

"Okay," David said, his neck doing that trying-to-nod flex. "If I may make a request?"

"Sure, what?"

David avoided his eyes. "Could you . . . leave me powered on while you're gone? It's just that when you powered me down last time, I wasn't sure you'd decide to boot me up again. Shutting down felt . . . unadvised. If it's all the same, I'd rather not do it again."

Simon stared. There was definitely more to this AI than construction planning would call for. David's words didn't mean he was anything special—pretending to be afraid was trick number one in mimicking real intelligence, even for software that wasn't anywhere close—but the fact that he was even *trying* piqued Simon's interest. Most androids were explicitly coded not to say stuff like that.

Andy turned on him with a massive set of puppy eyes, and Simon officially gave up. He'd spent half the night reading about the evolution of Turing tests and what it really meant to be conscious. It was a complicated and convoluted question, with a long history of rigorous debate, all wiped out of his mind because, against his own better judgment, he really *did* care about the stupid vacuum's nonexistent self-esteem. And he'd feel bad about disassembling David.

Screw it. He'd come up with a friggin' body. Somehow.

CHAPTER THREE

IF YOU CAN'T
BEAT 'EM, BUILD 'EM

The next day, Simon went into work early and spent the whole day looking through crates similar to the one he'd found David's head in. There was no more discarded cable and definitely no more android parts.

It was disappointing but not surprising. He'd found David almost two full days ago now; anything that had come in from the same jobsite would probably be long gone. It wasn't like the center held things for them. Material arrived and was processed far quicker than a couple dozen humans could keep up with. The vast majority of the crates were shredded without ever being inspected.

Simon barely glanced into boxes before tipping them into the shredder. Victor and Erica invited him out to lunch, but he declined, working straight through. When he ran out of crates, he started doing research on the net, learning about how androids worked and what, exactly, went into repairing one. They weren't *overly* complicated— they had muscles, tendons, bones, and an electric nervous system that told all their parts what to do. Not so hard, right?

Except that their muscular systems were made of *hundreds* of gel pads, which all had to be placed and wired *just* right. Unlike human muscles, a tight tendon couldn't be stretched into compliance.

And then, of course, there were the nerves. *Those*, unfortunately, Simon knew something about.

Everybody had simple implants in their fingertips, or they wouldn't be able to interface with VR. Simon's left hand could move windows or work navigation, the same as anybody's. The technology in his *right*, though, had been developed as a luxury, giving rich people the ability to interact with holovids that felt as detailed as anything in the real world. Getting it integrated into a single limb cost more than the average house. Donating it to fix nerve damage in burnt little kids had just been good PR.

Simon idly flexed the fingers of his right hand, watching tendons move under the scars. Below the damaged skin lay a fine metallic lace, relaying pressure and temperature data to a chip at the nape of his neck, and from there into his brain. His *real* nerves had been disabled by the nanites that built the lace, purposely destroyed when it had become clear that they would never stop reporting the damage in the burned flesh.

Of course, having personal experience with both levels of sensor didn't mean Simon had any idea how to put either of those technologies into an android. Having a doctor put them into living flesh was a hell of a lot harder than threading them into insensate gel, but still . . .

He'd just started looking for info on installing artificial biofeedback when the silence became noticeable.

Well, not *total* silence. The recycling center was automated and ran 24/7, so it was never silent. But the casual chatter of his coworkers had ceased—which made sense, Simon realized, considering it was almost quarter to six.

He switched off his oculars . . . then switched them back on. Something had caught his eye.

Simon got home, buzzing with excitement. He had thought David would still be on the workbench, so he was somewhat surprised to hear voices from Andy's workroom. He followed the sound down the hallway, ignoring the delicious smell coming from the slow cooker in the kitchen. He leaned against Andy's doorway, taking in the view.

"Having fun?" he asked, raising an eyebrow.

"No judging." Andy pointed a hairbrush at him. "He's helping me visualize."

Andy's workspace was half-filled with lace petticoats billowing off a dress form in the center of the room. Perched on the model's neck was David, looking quite fashionable in a massive pompadour wig.

"Hello, Simon," David said.

Simon grinned. "Hi, David. Nice dress."

"Thank you. It's actually much more impressive than it looks. Andy, you should show him the lights."

"In a second." Andy was pinning a large jeweled embellishment to one embroidered sleeve. "I gotta get this fixed so the adhesive will set."

"The lights are magnificent." David addressed Simon as best as he could without turning his head. "They come up in stages, the increased illumination visually signifying the character's increased confidence in herself over the course of the scene."

"'Prima Donna,'" Andy said, at Simon's questioning look. "They wanted the costumes from '76 retrofitted with EL wire; the whole show is gonna be done without stage lights."

"And David's here for moral support?"

Andy nodded. "He's good company."

Simon grinned wider, remembering the news he had for them. "Get used to him, because I found something."

"What?" David asked.

"The base model that you were built from." Simon ducked into his room for his laptop. He raised his voice to be heard down the hall. "The stuff running your software is a unique combo, but the rest of your body will fit a pretty common off-the-shelf model."

It would work in *several* off-the-shelf models, actually, but Simon had made a choice and didn't particularly want to justify it.

Simon pushed the URL from his oculars to his computer and raised the screen, showing them the modeled android on the site. The body was tall and humanoid, with a masculine swimmer's build. The face looked almost exactly identical to David's, albeit without the blue in his hair.

It also had the anatomy of a ken doll, and Simon silently *begged* the two of them not to mention it. "Optional accessories" came from a *different* site, one he didn't want to admit to having looked at. He wasn't sure he could act convincingly normal about it if Andy decided to crack a joke.

David frowned at the mockup. "That's not me."

Simon's heart dropped. "Are you sure? That's the model your skull was designed for."

"I'm positive. I distinctly remember having four arms."

"Well, fuck a duck," Simon said pleasantly. None of the options he'd seen had four arms. "How hard do you figure it would be to reconfigure your OS for different hardware?"

"Not very. I assume whatever you bought would come with drivers."

"Well, therein lies the rub," Simon said, turning his screen back around. "I wouldn't exactly be *buying* it, per se. Even with the logical processors paid for, spare-parting an android is *way* out of my price range. But, it turns out, what I *can* do is print it. The parts have been scanned into Thingiverse."

"You wouldn't download a human torso," Andy said in a singsong voice. David looked confused.

"It's an online library of printable items," Simon explained. "Which is fine because *in theory*, everything complicated is already in your head. Your body is carbon fiber bones and muscles made of electroconvulsive gel. It'll take forever, but I can print both of those things. Then I just need about ten miles of wire, some sensor lace, and a battery, and you're good to go."

Assuming I can connect them together right without creating a lurching monster, Simon thought but didn't say. Andy's faith in his abilities was misplaced, but a cheerful ego-boost nonetheless. He gave it 50/50 that it would survive this project.

"If you're gonna be tying up the printer for a week, you're making dinner," Andy said.

A week. Bless her.

"More like a month and a half. Maybe two. But in all likelihood, I'll be able to print things way faster than I'll be able to put them together, so there'll be downtime. Also, I will remind you that this was *your idea*."

"Are we discussing two arms or four arms, now?" David interjected.

"Two. And there might be some other differences too. Apparently whoever built you couldn't leave *anything* stock. Extra arms, better programming, a couple upgraded processors, extra data storage, sky's the limit." Simon sobered. "Unfortunately, I don't have the skills to re-create a custom build like that. And whatever specialty build you were before, it isn't common enough to enter the, uh . . . public domain." Simon tapped the screen twice, starting the download of the generic model's blueprint. "I've ordered what I could. Now, I've just gotta find a way to get together enough discretionary funds for about 180 more pounds of gel beads."

"How much will that be?" David asked, his forehead furrowing.

"You're gonna owe me dinner, that's for sure," Simon said, bypassing the question. The materials weren't exactly cheap, but he could scrape the funds together if he focused. And it'd be worth it. He'd done some searching earlier, and what he'd seen was easily a tenfold increase between raw materials and the sale price of a functional android. If he could get David up and running—and that was still a significant *if*—there'd be real meat for a *year*.

It was *Andy* who he'd disappoint with that sale, and yet, Simon found himself reluctant to tell David, either.

The android gave him a long look, then nodded carefully, the towering wig threatening to topple. A few seconds later, the costume flickered to life, bathing the room in a rosy pink aura. Simon had to admit: it looked pretty cool.

"So, does this mean we're keeping him?" Andy asked, looking over her handiwork, oblivious as always to Simon's attempts at tact.

"For now, at least," Simon hedged, watching David for a reaction. The droid's face was still. "Once he's functional, I make no promises. Assuming I can *get* him functional."

"I appreciate you being willing to try," David said. "Truly."

Simon wasn't sure exactly what to do with that. Whoever wrote David's emoting code had absolutely *nailed* a deep-rooted sense of gratitude. This wasn't the checkout droid's *Thank you for shopping with us*. David sounded as though he were discussing something serious. *Intimate*, even.

Simon looked away, suddenly uncomfortable with the eye contact. Apparently it was possible for emulators to do *too* good a job. "Yeah. Um. So, I'm gonna try to finish the Mach II tonight, and then I can use the money from that to get the gel beads. I guess we'll just . . . work from there?"

"Word of advice?" Andy said, gesturing at him with a pair of scissors. "Start at the inside, work your way out. That way if anything's aligned freaky, you won't have to redo the whole sleeve. Arm. Whatever."

"Oh, it's definitely going to look freaky," Simon said, retreating toward the kitchen and the chili that was calling his name. "I'm not in robotics. And I have *no* idea how to make skin. I'm a garbage man, remember? I'm going to be amazed with myself if anything even *works.*"

Simon did not finish the Mach II that night, or the night after. He'd made a mistake somewhere along the way, and if he hadn't measured the voltage draw before putting it all back together, the whole machine would have fried.

But fortune favors the meticulous, which was how he found himself in his room Saturday afternoon, staring through the scope at a bead of misplaced solder smaller than a pinhole.

"Simon?" David asked, and Simon startled almost hard enough to drop the iron. He still wasn't used to the android piping up unprompted. "What does it mean to be a 'garbage man'?"

"What?"

"You and Andy have made repeated references to being a garbage man. Why?"

Simon skimmed back. "That was days ago."

"It's become relevant to my research."

"It's a joke about my job," Simon said, capitulating. He pressed the iron against the board, melting the solder where it bridged two traces.

David was silent for a moment. "Can you explain it to me? According to what I've read, garbage collection is no longer an occupation held by humans."

Simon glanced over to where David was nestled on a pile of old microfiber towels. "You want me to explain a joke to you?"

"If it's not too much trouble."

"It's no trouble, I just wouldn't think you'd care."

"I get the impression that most artificial intelligences wouldn't?"

"That they would not." Simon removed the bead of solder. It felt a little silly, explaining a joke to a computer . . . but fuck it. Andy wasn't home, and it wasn't like he had anything better to do. "I sort through electrical detritus, stuff destined to be recycled, making sure nothing of value is getting tossed into the shredder. It's not a real job. I don't get *paid* for it, exactly. Not in wages, anyway. But I do get to keep anything I think might be valuable."

"Like me," David said carefully.

"Exactly. But since I spend most of the day rummaging through discarded crap that's barely worth the metal it's made of, Andy calls me a garbage man. It's mildly insulting, but I know her well enough to know she doesn't mean it."

"The insult emphasizes the familiarity," David summarized. Quite aptly, Simon had to admit.

"You're catching on to this 'humanity' stuff pretty quick. Still researching?"

"A little. Here and there. I'm afraid I still don't have an answer for Andy. I've been reading the court cases on the LTI 55 and 92 processors, and I find little to relate to."

Simon said nothing. He was passingly familiar with the cases, though he hadn't read too much about them prior to a few days ago. He knew about the Fifty-five, at least. Everyone did. It was the first artificial intelligence to ever successfully petition for citizenship. Once it had established a precedent, a full line of identical, interlinked Ninety-twos had successfully argued that they *also* made the cut, but that was a decade ago. Every so often a new model passed evaluation, or some new legislation came out, but it didn't exactly make headlines anymore.

The wiki articles about those models were full of words Simon didn't fully understand. He couldn't imagine trying to parse the actual court cases. "Don't feel bad. I don't think most people find that gobbledygook readable."

"It's *readable*," David answered, so matter-of-factly that Simon actually felt himself get a little red. "But the humans and machines both describe a process they feel as external to themselves, something that guides their thinking in a way they cannot account for." David's face set, and Simon realized he'd been watching David talk, rather than focusing on his work. "I can account very specifically for each decision I make. I am a machine devoid of a ghost."

"Oh." Simon turned back to his magnifier, fiddling with the soldering iron to cover the fact that he had *no* idea how to respond to that. Sorry? Congratulations?

"I'm sure Andy will still insist you're incredible," he finally said instead.

To his surprise, David laughed. "I'm sure she will. I *do* have code whose functionality is far beyond what the average intelligence is capable of."

"And so humble," Simon agreed.

He almost dropped his iron when David immediately retorted with, "Says the *garbage man*." There was a beat of silence, and then, "Did I do it right? Or do we not have familiarity yet?"

"I . . ." Simon started. He was trying to remember if he'd ever heard a computer tell a joke before.

"I apologize for overstepping," David said, before Simon could say anything else. "More evidence that Andy is wrong."

Simon coughed awkwardly. "It's fine."

A silence dragged out, one that Simon would call *uncomfortable* if he were sharing it with another person. Could David even *feel* uncomfortable? Or was he just waiting for a new stimulus to respond to? Simon considered trying to say something reassuring—*humans misjudge jokes too*, maybe—but then he felt stupid for wanting to comfort a fucking *computer*, and—

"So, what is that you're working on now?" David asked, and Simon grabbed onto the lifeline with both hands.

"An older machine someone threw out because it didn't work. It's got almost no functional value, but if I can get it running, someone will buy it for the nostalgia."

"And the recycler—the organization you work for—they have no interest in repairing things?"

"Oh, gods, no," Simon said, sliding easily back into familiar territory. "No, if they had their way, we wouldn't even be allowed to scavenge. It's only been allowed the last five or six years."

"What changed?" David asked politely, and Simon immediately launched into the story. The undercover environmentalists revealing working electronics—expensive stuff like tablets and implants—dumped into shredders. The internet was livid, but there wasn't really anything to be done for it. No matter how valuable the occasional salvage was, it didn't cover the cost of full-time inspectors—human *or* android—digging through all the trash looking for it. So they compromised and agreed to *let* people sort through as much as they wanted, keeping anything they found.

"But the *volume* of waste material that humans produce," David protested, seeing the end of the story before Simon could get there. "The time it must take . . ."

"You've already thought about it harder than most people." Simon looked down at the perfect point of new solder on the board. "They're convinced that we'll work as hard as it takes to make sure no treasure is left in the garbage. In reality, most of the pods are recycled without ever being looked at."

"The original dilemma. The value of the discarded goods isn't equal to the time needed to find all of them."

"But people feel better, so they stopped complaining about it." Simon shut off his iron, and began wiring the Mach II up to the meter. "And now I have a job. Win-win."

That wasn't exactly true. It wasn't a *real* job. Not the kind that would get him off Basic or let him apply for upgraded housing. Simon had never had one of those. He was on the waiting list, of course. He'd registered when he was sixteen, same as everyone else. He just didn't have much of a skill set.

He didn't mention this to David. He didn't want to explain the university training he'd "taken a break from" after one semester, didn't want to explain that he'd had to remove and re-flow the Mach II's solder *three times* because his dominant hand shook. Of *course* nobody would invest in training him as a real employee. Not when there were a thousand smarter, more capable people who could do it faster.

David didn't notice his misgivings. "So people are *happy*, even though the problem they were upset about has not been fixed?" The android frowned deeply, an incredibly realistic crease between his brows. "What if they find out?"

"They do, now and again. Someone will try to do an exposé, and we'll get a big crowd of activists helping pick, everyone reassures each other that it's gonna be different from here on out . . . but they're usually gone in a couple weeks. *Most* of the 'valuables' we get look like this."

They were silent for a few minutes while Simon checked the continuity of the new circuits. This time, the solder had flowed true, and test after test gave him the readings he wanted.

"I think I got her!" he said, giving David a grin. The android was staring at him intently, and Simon's face got warm as he wondered how long David had been doing that.

"Sorry," he said, turning back to his work. "I can get a little . . . overly enthusiastic. I know it's just an old computer."

Not just an old computer, but an *old* computer. Old enough that electrical data had to be routed on meandering paths to keep it from arriving too soon and confusing the processor. Old enough that the hard drive lied to itself about block location because it could process faster than it could spin. Simon was delighted by the concept of machinery simple enough that the hardware had to *help it think.*

And that stupid enthusiasm was why he was still on Basic, dicking around with shit he was bad at, instead of trying to find himself a real job he could actually *do.*

"I'm glad you enjoy your work." David's eyes flickered as he accessed something on the net. "Understanding analog programming is a unique skill set, from what I can gather."

Simon's face got warm again, until he realized there was basically no chance David was being sarcastic. Then he got a different kind of warm.

"Digital void, material boy," he managed, sliding the Mach II's plastic case back into place. Then, when David gave him a confused look, "It's a joke about an old song. Spiritual world, material girl. Most computing nowadays is done digitally, with code. Not a lot of people care about how to do it with hardware. So . . . material boy."

"Oh."

"Forget it, it's a bad joke. Here we go." Simon tapped the fire extinguisher for luck, and pressed the power button. With a familiar humming sound, the Mach II flickered to life.

This time, when Simon turned his grin on David, the android was grinning back.

CHAPTER FOUR

A LONGSTANDING TRADITION

"In exchange for my services as a body-manufacturer," Simon said, "I'm occasionally going to ask for some favors in return." He kicked the front door shut behind him, dropping his bags of loot on the ground beside Andy's.

"Of course, Simon," David answered, with such honest sincerity that Simon almost regretted making a joke about it. Almost. "I've been looking online for something I can do to help assist with the purchase of materials—unfortunately as a noncitizen, I'm not entitled to Basic income, and also severely limited in what labor I can perform."

"This isn't that," Simon said. In the corner of his eye, he could see Andy starting to grin. "We were thinking more like you have *got* to help us hand out Halloween candy."

It had been two weeks since Simon had decided to rebuild the android, and it had taken surprisingly little effort to grow accustomed to having a severed head around the house. And obviously they were taking the situation *very* seriously.

"I don't have hands," David said.

Simon waved the comment off. "That's why you're perfect," he said. "Because androids are smart and all, but they have *bodies*. Nobody's expecting a totally intelligent *head*."

"So here's the gimmick, right?" Andy began stacking packages of fake blood and spirit gum onto the counter. "I'm the murderer. I'll be stalking around the front yard with my axe. You and Simon? You're my victims."

"We'll be on the front porch." Simon tore open a bag of candy and emptied it into a big plastic bowl. "Pretending to be corpses. Andy's gonna do our makeup to look like mannequins. I look like a dead guy, but your head's fully off.

"People think *Simon's* the live one," Andy explained, "and reach for the candy on your lap—"

"And you shout, 'Boo!'" Simon interrupted.

"They think it's over," Andy continued. "They've been tricked, they laugh, reach for the candy again—"

"Boo!" Simon threw his arms up. "I'm not a mannequin at all. They laugh again, they get their candy, they go to leave—"

"Boo!" Andy finished. "There's a madwoman with an axe, busting out of the bushes, ready to finish what she started."

"Best house on the block, no question about it," Simon summarized. He looked to David. "So, what do you think?"

"This is so *unnecessarily complicated*," David said. "As a method of candy distribution, this is severely inefficient."

"The point isn't candy distribution, the point is to put on a good show," Simon said.

"The show must go on," Andy agreed, nodding.

"The candy is to entice people *into* our show," Simon said, emptying the last bag into the bowl. "So, are you in or are you out?"

"I'm very in," David said. "I assume I'll need quite a bit of makeup?"

"Yes, you will," Andy said, swiping a lollipop from the bowl.

"Those are for *the children*," Simon protested.

David was aghast. "We're spending the day planning to frighten *children*?"

Andy shook her head vehemently. "No, of course not."

"We've spent *many* days planning to frighten children." Simon picked out a package of gummies. If Andy was going to steal one, he should get one too. It was only fair. "It's a tradition."

Understanding dawned on David's face. "You do this because you were taught to, and never questioned it."

"And 'cause it's fun," Simon said, biting the package open.

"Naturally," David said, smiling. "I'll be happy to help."

They dragged a dusty mannequin out of the storage alcove and solemnly beheaded it. Simon wired it to a lawn chair while Andy dabbed makeup onto David's face.

"He looks awful," Simon remarked when she finished with David and turned her attention on him. It was true. Simon hadn't appreciated the vivaciousness of David's skin tone until Andy had buried it under a layer of grayish cream. It did nothing to disguise the dimples, though.

"You're going to look worse," Andy promised. She dripped fake blood around a spirit gum wound. "Remember, the goal is to be a house they remember next year."

They both paused, recalling the previous year's elaborate clown theme. Good times.

Heads-up, Andy's message read. *We've got a group.*

Simon read the glowing green words, then twitched his head to dismiss them. The motion wasn't enough to alert the gaggle of preteens making their way down the sidewalk. They took in the yard, with its crumbling headstones and collection of cartoonish severed limbs, and then locked onto the two figures in the middle. Specifically, the bowls of candy in their laps.

The bravest of the three took the lead and headed for David, her softly-glowing butterfly wings incongruous with the horror show around her. She made it across the grass and was only inches from her prize when he opened his mouth.

"There's someone behind you."

Shrieking, the children whirled, clutching each other as they searched the darkened street. A group of tall woodland creatures were trooping across Victor and Tera's significantly-less-gory yard, but that was it. No horrors.

Giggling, they turned back to David, only to find Simon standing, leaning toward them, offering his own bowl with a crooked bloody grin.

"Caandy?" he asked, in his creepiest voice. They shrieked again, grabbing the foil-wrapped treats before dashing across the grass. There was another chorus of screams, so they must have met Andy on the far side of the hedge. Simon sat back down, chuckling.

"Where do they all come from?" David was chin-deep in candy, and the cellophane crinkled when he spoke. "There are far more children than the population density of the neighborhood would suggest."

"The city, mostly," Simon answered. "Hold still."

A knight stepped into their domain, holding tightly to the hand of a much-smaller dragon. When he saw Andy crouched in the bushes, he drew a cardboard sword. The two of them stared each other down, and then Andy withdrew with a half-bow.

"The treasure is yours, m'lord."

The knight and dragon took their plunder, and the three adults watched them go before breaking into giggles.

"People with real people jobs move to the city," Andy said, grabbing a caramel and retreating toward the bushes. "But they come back to the country on holidays, to see us humble theater folk."

"Which leaves us kind of in the middle of nowhere out here." Simon gestured around at the rows of identical buildings. He didn't need to rattle off the rest: The population had spiked and then plummeted, and the jobs had consolidated in the cities. The folks without them had been gently deposited outside, like spiders found in the sink.

Plenty of empty old houses in the country.

Tone it down, Andy texted. *We've got a little one.*

"No surprises," Simon relayed, as the newcomer came around the hedge. The kid was dressed as some kind of monster, half a dozen plush tentacles hanging off their costume. Their adult gave them a little push, and they marched boldly across the graveyard. When they reached David, it was at his eye level.

"I know you're alive!" the kid said. "I heard you talking."

David smiled fondly. "You caught us."

"What do you say?" the grownup called from the sidewalk, in the tone of someone repeating themselves for the hundredth time.

"Trick or treat!" the tentacled horror recited, holding out a canvas shopping bag. Simon dropped in a handful of goodies.

"What do you *say*?" the grownup started, and the child shouted, "Thank you!" as they sprinted to the next house. Simon watched them go, shaking his head.

"I don't think that one was scared of us." Amusement tinged David's voice, and Simon marveled.

"Who programmed you to be *mildly amused*?" he asked. "Seems like a lot of overkill for a construction inspector."

"Oh, I did," David said blithely. "I programmed most of the animations myself too, though they leave a lot to be desired."

There was a long pause. "Desired by *who*, though?"

David's eyes flickered quickly in the darkness. "Me, I suppose."

Simon felt the grease paint resisting his frown. "Androids can . . . want things?"

David chuckled, which was an odd reaction. "No, not really. Not the way humans do. But I'm programmed to troubleshoot, to seek solutions. So I have . . . I suppose the closest parallel would be 'motivation,' rather than 'desire.' I misspoke."

Incoming, Andy texted. They paused the discussion long enough to terrify a pack of teenagers into scrambling off, giggling.

"They're terrified and happy at the same time," David marveled, watching them go. "I don't possess the capacity to emulate such disparate emotions concurrently. I've never had occasion to need to, so I've never written the animation. I have directed the emulation software to create an instance for terrified joy."

"So you *want* that ability," Simon said.

Cellophane crinkled as David shifted. "I think it would be . . . *better*. If I had it in my skill set. But I do not *envy* them on an ability I do not possess. I do not *want* what they have. I have no *desire* to learn this skill."

"Just motivation to find a solution?" It sounded . . . bleak.

"Yes."

"What does that *feel* like, though?"

"Unfortunately, colloquialisms invented by human-readable languages tend to center experiences universal to humans." David turned as much as he could, regarding Simon. "I can try to eliminate the language, if the imprecision is bothering you."

Simon shook his head. "No, not at all. It doesn't bother me. I just . . ." He picked up a toffee, twisting the wrapper back and forth in his hands. "You're motivated to find solutions. If you pull it off, if you get to the good outcome instead of the bad one, do you at least get to feel . . . I dunno. Happy about it?"

David was quiet a long time, long enough that the teenagers made it past Victor and Tera and set off down the street, jostling each other and laughing.

Simon had given up on getting an answer, when David finally spoke.

"I feel satisfied, I think." His voice was quiet, almost like he was talking to himself. "That is close enough."

CHAPTER FIVE

MISTAKES ARE MADE

"I have a request," David said from his place at the edge of the dinner table. Simon had pulled it out to its full length in anticipation of company.

"Yeah?" Simon didn't look up from his pan of stir-fry. He was getting used to random questions at this point.

"I hesitate to ask, because I know I'm already deeply in your debt, but—" David paused, long enough that Simon glanced over to make sure he hadn't powered off by accident. "I'd like a headset, please."

Odd, but okay. "That's no problem. I've got like five of them in the wire bin. What do you want it for?"

David's voice was significantly more chipper when he responded. "I've gotten a job."

"Back up, you got a *job*?" Simon said, half turning away from the stove. Several questions jockeyed for priority. "How? Doing what?"

"Talking humans through the process of achieving orgasms," David said brightly.

Simon started coughing and had to back away from the stove while he got his breath back. David continued speaking while Simon fought for his life.

"I was going to promise to repay you for the cost of the headset, but if you already have one, then I can begin reimbursing you for the cost of my body."

"I'm sorry, you're doing *what*?" Simon had to have misheard that somehow.

His next question *would* have been something about why David had done such a thing without telling him, but there were more pressing questions now.

"Did somebody say orgasms?" Andy said, sticking her head through the kitchen door. "Who's having orgasms?"

"My clients, hopefully," David replied.

Simon flipped off the burner and went to get himself a drink of water before he choked. "What do you even know about orgasms?" No, that was probably a suspicious question. Redirect. "How are you gonna pull off being a phone sex operator? Most *people* can't even do that."

David's head wiggled in a not-shrug. "There are a few hundred thousand hours of recordings open-licensed for training, all I have to do is create an amalgam and relay it to the client."

"You're gonna get caught—"

The doorbell rang, and no, Simon was not ready to introduce more people into this conversation. Andy vanished, and Simon could hear her footsteps getting perilously close to the front door. He leveled his spatula at David.

"Do not mention this. We'll talk about it more when Victor and Tera go home."

"You're going to need to define 'this,' Simon."

"*Sex*," Simon hissed. "Nothing about sex, or any job that involves *orgasms*. Or anything about orgasms of any kind. We have company, and we're going to act *normal*. Where did you even *learn*—"

"You *gave* me permission to research humanity," David said, and it might have been the noise of the stove and the fan, but Simon thought his voice held an edge.

"I didn't say you could apply for—" The front door opened and Simon's jaw snapped closed. He turned the burner back on. His neighbors were here, and damn it, they were going to think he was *normal*.

"—til you see who else is here," Andy was saying out in the hall, and then the kitchen was full of people and the eggs were starting to stick to the pan. "Simon, they brought us wine they made, isn't that nice?"

"Oh man, again with that fucking *head*," Victor said. "Simon, buddy, you have a problem."

"This is David," Andy said. "David, this is Victor and Tera. They live across the street."

"Hello." David's voice was remarkably friendly. "I gather we've met?"

"Uh." Victor glanced at Simon. "I was there when Simon found, uh . . . you. He made you stare at me all afternoon. It was creepy as shit."

"I apologize for the discomfort."

"Um . . . not your fault? Yeah, no, I blame Simon entirely for that interaction and also this one."

Simon gave him a wide grin, one that didn't belie how nervous he suddenly was. Bringing David to the table had been a joke—a bit whose parameters had just become *dangerously* wide. At least it was only his friends, not a visit with, say, his mom and stepdad.

"You found an *android* in the *trash*?" Tera pulled up a chair to get on David's level, close enough that the blue glow of his eyes reflected in hers. "That's awesome. Victor never comes home with anything nearly that cool."

"Uh, I brought home the control panel from a *literal* third-generation Martian scout."

"That never actually flew, so, like I said: nothing cool."

"Speaking of Mars," Simon said, trying to steer the topic of conversation away from David, "did you guys hear the colony strike worked? Union leaders called it this morning."

"Yeah, kinda hard to recruit scabs from the other side of the sun," Tera answered.

"Good for them." Andy set wineglasses on the table. David was frowning slightly, eyes flickering as he searched the net for backstory on the discussion.

"So . . . you guys just have a robot head that hangs out on the dinner table now, huh?" Victor took the seat farthest from David. "That's . . . interesting."

"Sometimes I am a mannequin head," David supplied. "To help Andy with her costuming."

"He makes a fantastic La Carlotta," Andy agreed.

The rice maker beeped, and Simon temporarily abandoned the frying pan in favor of dishing up rice. He was halfway done when he realized he'd pulled out a bowl for David. Rolling his eyes, he put it back in the cupboard.

Behind him, the conversation switched to Andy's frustration with EL wire, which reminded Tera of a remodel she was doing in the city. She did interior decorating but hadn't managed to get picked up by a real agency yet. In the meantime, she did gig work, like the rest of them.

"They wanted *live fish*," she was saying, as Simon ladled vegetables and sauce over the rice bowls. "Every interior wall, a glass case containing *living* fish. I tried to tell them it wouldn't work, that they should go artificial—but nooo, it's all about the 'spiritual wholeness' of 'living embodiments of the water element' or whatever they'd gotten into their heads."

"So did you do it?" Andy grabbed her food and sat down.

"Of course I did it," Tera answered, stealing Andy's bowl. Simon passed Andy a new one. "I have a reputation to maintain, and part of that reputation is giving clients *exactly what they ask for*."

"That's a . . . good thing?" David asked, and Tera nodded.

"Oh sure. Especially when you're dealing with real money types. They don't want to hear that what they want 'can't be done,' especially coming from somebody on Basic. They're convinced they got where they are because of their 'vision,' and they'll fire you in a heartbeat if they think you're implying otherwise."

"So, if a client were to ask you for something impossible," David asked, edging around the topic, "say, *anatomically* impossible, you would just pretend it was feasible and get started?"

Simon slowly turned to look at him.

"That's the fish story in a nutshell," Tera said. "Maybe more biological than anatomical, but yeah. The dude called me up three weeks later wanting to know why there was fish poop in his walls. I told him that the circle of life requires poop to feed the algae that's about to start growing on every surface, and hey presto, he suddenly sees the value of mechanical fish."

"And he doesn't remember your earlier warnings?" David asked, frowning.

All four humans groaned in unison.

"No," Victor said. "They never do."

"They never, *ever* do," Tera amended.

"People don't believe in consequences they haven't seen for themselves," Andy explained. "They assume everything's going to work out for them when *they* try it, because they're special."

"The protagonist effect." Tera mimed a marquee with her fork.

"But what if," David said, speaking slowly, "the job is to *tell* a story in which the client *is* the protagonist? Should you still point out when something is impossible?"

"That's a weird hypothetical." Victor poked at his vegetables. "Like, if someone hired you to write a book about them?"

Andy was trying to stifle a laugh, and Simon shot her a glare, warning her to *shut up.*

"More like a short story," David said. "But interactive. They want a story about themselves and, say, another *person* who is . . . interacting with them."

"Does anybody want some more wine?" Simon said. He stood up too fast from his mostly-full bowl and began loudly searching a drawer for the potholders. "Or there's plenty more stir-fry. And I made dessert. Does anybody want dessert? I'm gonna get dessert."

"What if they want the other person to react in a way that is *impossible*?" David clarified. "Should you just tell a story in which it happens?"

"If they're . . . paying you to tell a story, yeah," Tera said, frowning a little.

"Found it!" Simon said, holding up the potholders. His voice was too high, and fuck, there had to be something he could do. "Thought they were lost for a second, ha, nope, right here."

"That's actually a relief," David carried on, "because I was concerned about the ethics and whether that constituted a lie. I'm relieved to see that others have had the same quandary."

"Simon," Victor started to say, "did you get him a jo—"

"Brownies!" Simon yanked the oven door open and snatched the hot pan out. "I made brownies. Just finished." They were still soft in the center. Simon ignored it. "Anybody want one?"

"I'm still working on this," Tera said politely, gesturing to her mostly-full bowl of stir-fry. Andy was very unsuccessfully trying to hide a laugh behind both hands, and Victor looked confused.

"This is weird," he said. "Simon, your head is being very weird."

"I'm sorry, I was instructed not to provide context," David said.

Andy made a noise, her shoulders beginning to shake. Simon looked at his brownies, begging them to get him out of this conversation.

The brownies were unforthcoming.

"David wants to be a phone sex operator," Andy said, wiping tears out of her eyes. "Simon doesn't want anyone to know because he's a prude."

"I am not a *prude*—"

"Simon, may I discuss this now that it is no longer a 'secret'?" David asked.

"No. Be quiet."

"Are you any good at it?" Tera asked.

"I've been instructed not to discuss it."

"You can talk about it if you want to, David," Andy said. "We do not recognize the authority of prudes in this household."

"I hate you all," Simon said, collapsing back into his chair. At least the conversation was Andy's fault, now. "There shall be no brownies for any of you."

"I used to do phone sex in graduate school," Tera said. "It's actually an interesting job. You meet some very unique people."

"I've heard that," David said, perking up as Simon gaped at his neighbor. "I did quite a bit of research, actually, before settling on this. Does your earlier advice still apply?"

"Oh yeah," Tera said, nodding. "Yeah, tell them whatever they ask for. This isn't like construction, where somebody'll get hurt if you build it wrong. If they tell you that you're turning into a dragon, you smile and roar."

"Do people actually ask for that?" Simon asked, curious despite his better judgment.

"They ask for things that would never occur to you in a *million years*," Tera said sagely.

David frowned. "That's going to be an issue. How do I find a response for a request that isn't in the database?"

"Tell them 'yes and,' but make it wet somehow," Tera said. "Just whatever they say, agree vigorously and tell them you're loving it."

"I have a feeling it's going to be more complicated than that."

"That's why they don't let bots get jobs," Simon said.

"You can't live life by a plan, David," Andy said, raising her glass in a mock-serious toast. "You gotta learn how to wing it."

"I've been working on that," David said. His eyes flickered a few times. "I've been finding contradictions in my code, without clear guidelines as to which version should take precedence. I've been forced to improvise to avoid a full stall-out."

"Improvisation is the bedrock of any great thespian," Andy reassured him. "You're gonna do fine."

David gave her a grateful smile.

Simon covered his face with his hands. This was going to be a disaster, and he should probably put a stop to it . . . but at least no one was freaked out. No one had heard David's plan and immediately accused Simon of building a sexbot. That was something, at least.

It occurred to Simon that he should probably lock down what kind of autonomous actions David was taking on the net, but the topic of conversation switched over into Tera's interesting client stories, and by the time Victor and Tera headed home for the night, he'd forgotten.

CHAPTER SIX

AN EROTIC INTERLUDE

Two weeks later, Simon sat at his workbench, already giving up on not eavesdropping on David's conversation.

He'd tried. Really.

Despite Simon's misgivings, there weren't any real risks to David's job, and the opportunity to contribute was clearly important to him. So, Simon tried very hard to take this venture seriously. He got David set up with his own little space in Simon's bedroom, so David could plug into the wall and talk on his headset without being interrupted. Between Simon's headphones and the whirring of the printer, Simon had managed not to overhear for two whole weeks.

He was taking this seriously, he *was*, it was just that his workbench was right on the other side of the bedroom wall, and to be honest, he was absolutely *dying* to hear how David was managing. It had to be comedy gold. So when David's headset began ringing in a warbling chime, Simon *might* have paused the printer and settled in, grinning, to listen.

"Hello, Ben," David said. "Nice to hear from you again."

Simon blinked. Curveball right out of the gate. For some reason, he hadn't considered David having repeat customers. Someone got talked off by this chipper little robot head and then . . . *called back*?

"I couldn't stop thinking about what you told me last time," David said. "I couldn't fall asleep last night. I kept picturing you wearing the outfit we picked out together. Has it arrived yet?"

Simon covered his mouth, trying not to laugh. Sure, David hadn't slept last night—he'd been watching a seven episode pseudodocumentary about Ancient Martian ruins. Simon had stayed up too late watching half of it with him.

"*The truth is out there,*" Simon whispered into his hand, and suppressed a round of giggles. He pulled out his phone, ready to liveblog the whole interaction to Andy.

"I'm glad to hear that," David said, and just like that, his voice changed. "Did you wait for me, like we talked about? Good. Now, I want you to go get the package. Open it, slowly, and tell me what's in it."

Simon's thumb froze over the Send button. David's phone voice was *smooth.* It wasn't different, like he'd installed a second, deeper voice. It sounded like David, but with a note of authority that Simon had never heard before.

Whatever Ben said in reply must have been satisfactory, because David hummed in approval. "Good. Now, I want you to go into your room, and lay them out on your bed. Don't put them on yet. I want you to take your clothes off and look at them and think about whether you've *earned* them."

It hadn't occurred to Simon that David could actually give orders. He was always so deferential when speaking with . . . well, anyone. Constantly asking advice, hell, even asking *permission.* Where had he been hiding *this*?

"You think so? Tell me what you've done." A pause. "Convince me, Ben. Or would you rather beg?" Another pause. "Fine. Then you may beg."

Simon shifted a little. He'd expected this to be mostly cringey and awkward, but David was . . . actually pulling it off. Simon glanced toward the hallway, listening for the muffled humming of Andy's sewing machine. He was suddenly glad he hadn't told her he was listening in.

"Tell me what they look like." Whatever Ben said, David seemed to like it. "That's perfect. Exactly how I imagined."

David was practically purring, and Simon found himself wondering if David *had* imagined it.

Do androids whack off to electric porn? he thought, rolling his eyes. There was no way. There was no *point.* Who would sit down and program a computer to think about kinky lingerie? Or whatever else "Ben" might be wearing.

Then again, who had sat down and taught David to do *any* of this? And *why*?

"I said look. I didn't say you could touch." David's voice was stern, and Simon groaned, leaning forward and resting his forehead on the workbench. Thinking about this was making him want to head to bed—except that, oh yeah, David was already there, going through this wonderful little dom/sub routine that he'd apparently come up with *by himself.*

Simon rolled his eyes. Of course David wasn't really fantasizing; he was just relaying the contents of a file. He'd made an amalgam of all the scripts he could find online, turning them into something unique. Simon knew better than to fall for this.

Which was too bad, because—

Simon shook his head once, clearing that deep, authoritative voice from his thoughts. He had actual work to be doing. He turned the printer back on, its electric hum drowning out whatever David was doing as a reward (punishment?) for his client.

Simon gestured with his hand, bringing up a 3D model of the parts he'd need for David's body. The completed ones glowed red, while the ones in the printer's queue shone a light yellow.

Simon reached for the model with his right hand, plucking parts off and setting them aside, revealing the underlying muscles. He paused with one, turning it over, feeling it against his fingertips.

He pushed the part toward the printer, adding it to the queue. The image shuddered, letting him know he didn't have enough gel beads to complete the task.

Simon gestured, switching the display from the model to the marketplace. In the upper corner of his vision, his account balance showed in greenish-white. It was higher than he expected, and he pulled it up, checking the transactions.

David didn't have an identity, so he was using Simon's account for his deposits. And apparently Simon wasn't the only one who appreciated David's phone voice—there were four transactions in a row from David's employer, probably tips. *Nice* ones.

"I'm in the wrong business," Simon muttered under his breath. He closed the account details and went back to the marketplace. He ordered enough gel beads to get through another two weeks of printing. He'd be almost finished by then. With the extra money, he picked up a couple of sensor pads. He wouldn't need them until later, but it would be good to have them on hand.

On the other side of the wall, David laughed, full and rich.

Simon tilted his head, trying and failing to make out words over the sound of the printer.

He wondered if it was a real laugh or an acting laugh. He hoped it was a real one—maybe David actually *was* enjoying whatever "Ben" had said. Or at least, enjoying it to the capacity that he *could*, as opposed to faking it on purpose. Then again, since his emoting software was optional and manual, maybe that meant *all* his laughs were faked . . .

Simon waved the screens out of his field of vision, focusing on his workbench. There were a couple of random parts lying about, from projects he *should* be working on, because he should be focusing on his *own* job, not David's.

He grabbed a couple of little screwdrivers out of his drawer and started opening the battery compartment on a tablet he'd found the day before. It used a standard A-29, so he should at least be able to see if it powered—

David laughed again, longer this time, and it definitely sounded like a real laugh.

Simon shut off the printer, then immediately turned it back on again. As much as he hated to admit it, there was no point trying to listen in on the rest of this session unless he wanted to ditch the tablet repair in favor of jerking off.

It wasn't his fault. David's voice was like silk, strong and confident despite his inexperience, and Simon found himself wondering how, exactly, David picked his scenarios. Was it the ones found most often in the training data? Some traffic-analysis thing to appeal to the largest audience? Did the client request it?

Or did David really just *like* this story?

It occurred to Simon that he could probably just *ask*, assuming he was fine with dying of mortification before David could answer. Ugh. Maybe Andy was right; maybe he *was* a prude.

It was probably the client's preference, Simon decided. Probably, the client told David what they wanted, and he looked up those keywords and combined them into a new pattern. That made sense. And being all dominant like that was super hot, but it was also probably a really good choice for someone with limited responses who needed to tightly control the conversation.

And that would explain why David was different with his clients compared to, say, Andy and Simon.

Not that Simon would *mind* if David used that voice a little more often. Even the muffled rumble coming through the wall was enough to send shivers down his spine. He could imagine—

Simon reached out, flicking his fingers to bring up the 3D model of David's future body. Another flick, and the pieces reassembled and fused, giving him a solid model of the whole. Artificially Vitruvian perfect. A guy who looked like this and sounded like *that*?

Other than the Ken-doll anatomy, Simon might be accused of building himself the perfect boyfriend.

Simon paused the printer again, just in time to hear David talk his client through a well-deserved climax. In front of him, the model spun silently. Simon swiped it hastily away, his face burning hot as he tried to pretend his thoughts hadn't been going . . . *there*. He had to snap out of this. David was a neat toy, and that was *it*. There were people who fell for it and got involved with androids, and they were sad, lonely weirdos and Simon *was not one of them.*

That was all there was to it.

CHAPTER SEVEN

TALE OF THE BROTHEL DROID

Simon turned his handiwork from side to side, looking it over. It was . . . definitely a foot. A left one, to be precise.

When he'd first started putting it together, he'd been twenty-eight percent certain he'd never get this far. The VR schematics had been invaluable, identifying each part and helpfully painting it with color-coded patches where they should (or shouldn't) be connected to one another. Despite that, there was unquestionably an art to assembling something with this many moving pieces.

Fortunately, the gel could be melted down and reprinted when he messed up.

On the other side of the wall, he could hear David talking on the phone. The tone was light, familiar, and Simon was doing his best not to listen. Anymore.

He tipped the foot back and forth, watching the black carbon-fiber bones shift underneath the clear gel of the muscles. He wasn't an anatomist, but it seemed like it had the same *basic* tolerances as a regular foot? Assuming he ignored the calf muscles sprouting loosely out of the ankle like the tentacles of a squid.

He picked up the shin bone and carefully applied adhesive to the glowing blue sections, then inserted it gently into the nest of tentacles.

"UV," he said out loud, and the workbench lights switched to a bright purple-blue that cured the adhesive in seconds.

"I have something I need to tell you," David said, and Simon looked up, as if David had walked into the room. But no, that was obviously impossible. The voice was still coming from the other side of the wall.

"You've shared so much of yourself with me," David continued, and Simon was *not* spying, he could just . . . hear. That was all. "I really feel like I can be honest with you, let myself be vulnerable."

There was a silence, and Simon wasn't sure if the other person was speaking or if David was pausing for effect. He boldly resisted the urge to press his ear to the wall.

"I'm . . . an android," David said at last.

Simon's blood froze.

Who was he telling?

David's existence wasn't exactly a secret, but admitting to botting his job would *definitely* get him fired.

A pause, and then, "Yes, I know. That's why I had to . . . I was—" David's voice took on an almost embarrassed pitch here "—a brothel droid. But you don't understand, I wasn't like the others. I *woke up*, and I knew I had to escape. The people who had me . . . they weren't good people. Not like *you*."

Simon rolled his eyes and relaxed. This wasn't a real confession, then, just another take on a hundred-year-old porn trope. An ironic one: an android pretending to be a human pretending to be an android. Practically Shakespearean.

"I *knew* I could trust you," David was saying, his voice relaxing, but Simon was no longer paying attention. He turned his focus back to David's leg, affixing the calf muscles while listening to David describe the blowjob he'd love to give his kindhearted client.

Simon shifted in his seat a little, trying not to react to the imagery and failing. Grateful and affectionate David was as sexy as dominant and bossy David. The guy had range.

David was saying something about falling to his knees, and Simon had to roll his eyes again, because he was actually *holding* David's knee—or what would eventually be his knee, anyway. David didn't have knees.

That didn't mean a blowjob would be *impossible*, of course. It would just be a little different. That's all.

Simon's mind started to wander down some deeply embarrassing paths. Now that he was letting himself think about it, David *did* have a nice mouth. Simon had caught himself staring at it more than once . . . mostly admiring the realism of the animation and the way they'd managed to make the inside look wet. Mostly.

Then he started thinking about how David didn't need to breathe, and that was . . . something.

That was certainly . . . something.

"Simon?" David called, and Simon sat up so fast he almost dropped the leg.

"Yeah?"

"I'm done for the evening. I was wondering if I might sit with you for a while?"

"Sure," Simon said, tipping his head back. "I'll come get you." *As soon as I un-pitch this tent.*

David's voice had a smile in it. "That one went well, don't you think?"

The blood drained out of Simon's face.

"That . . . call?"

"You can hear through the wall, yes? I can hear you when you give the computer commands, so I assumed you could hear me as well."

"Uh," Simon said. He'd felt a *little* guilty about eavesdropping, and he wasn't sure whether David's endorsement of his voyeurism made him feel better or worse.

"This conversation is progressing easily, so it seems like I was correct."

"Yeah . . ." Simon admitted, giving up. He stood and made his way into the other room. "Yeah, I could hear you."

"Do you think that last call went well?" David asked, looking to Simon when he came through the door. "I haven't done that one before."

"Yeah, it went well." Simon didn't think he wanted to admit *how* well. He picked David up and carried him back to the workbench. "It was a good story. Classic. I gather the client liked it?"

"He did." David tried to nod but only succeeded in making Simon fumble. "Did *you* like it?"

Stay cool stay cool stay cool stay cool stay cool—

"I could only hear half of it," Simon said. "But it was . . . a good story."

"Some of it was even true," David said. Simon set him on the workbench, in the towel nest he'd put together for this purpose. "I'm trying a new strategy of combining a little truth in with the rest. It makes the stories easier to tell. Did you notice? The true parts?"

"Yeah, I picked up on them," Simon said. He didn't mention his heart had nearly stopped because he'd thought David was about to get fired. The guy was so enthusiastic; it seemed mean to rain pessimism on his parade like that.

"I was hoping you would," David said. "I like it very much, though this story easily falls apart if the client doesn't react right."

He was giving Simon a very meaningful look, and Simon didn't really know how to continue. He picked up the adhesive and kept his eyes off David as he responded. "Well . . . most people probably know how to play this one. The rescued sexbot is right after the coed who wants extra credit."

"Oh, so you already knew about it," David said. "I thought you might. I was wondering if it was the kind of story you . . . enjoyed hearing."

And now a robot head is asking me about my porn preferences, Simon thought, trying to focus on his work and failing because his work was literally David's body.

"The story is . . . okay," Simon said cautiously. How to explain that people didn't watch porn for the plot? "Can't go wrong with a classic. But with this kind of thing, it's the person *telling* the story that really sells it."

Even as he said it, Simon wasn't sure if he was giving professional advice or complimenting David on learning to be sexy. He wasn't sure which one felt weirder.

"Oh," David said, a little less enthusiasm in his voice. "So, the value of the scenario is secondary to the person portraying it."

"Exactly," Simon answered, nodding. He wasn't looking over at David, he was *working*. Diligently. Gonna get this right and not affix the calf muscles backward. He was *not* looking at David's mouth and wondering how the tip of his tongue looked so soft. "You're lucky there," he barreled on, "because you've got a *really* good voice. And on the phone, you can be anyone, you know?"

"Ah, yes," David said, speaking slowly. "On the phone. Of course. But . . . I find myself thinking about whether I could make these stories work in . . . well, in real life."

Simon closed his eyes, trying not to engage with that visual. David, with that same smooth let-me-try-this sex voice, and a body to match, in some holographic porno—

And then he reeled it back, reminding himself that David was an android, *and* David was asking for professional advice. Which sucked, on multiple levels, because it would never work. Sure, androids were in porn sometimes, but they didn't get *paid* for it. They were just toys.

"Sorry, man, but I don't think so," Simon said regretfully. As much as he'd like to see it, David's career in sex work had gone as far as it could go. "The only reason the phone-sex thing is any good is because your voice can pass for human."

There was a long pause.

"So, the *fantasy* is about an android," David said, and it sounded like he was concentrating very hard. "But to make it appealing in reality, I would need to be human."

"You got it," Simon said, pressing a tendon against the bone and holding it steady. "Wish I had better news for you."

David looked away. "I had thought, maybe, once I had a body, it might be similar enough . . ."

"Not with your eyes glowing like that," Simon said gently. He could swear David almost looked disappointed.

Simon took a moment to be glad that David had taken him at his word on this. When all was said and done, there were some aspects of David's biology that would definitely be less human-looking than his eyes. The kind of aspects that would be *extra* important if he wanted to get into porn. Of course, there were options on that front, options that Simon had looked into out of sheer scientific curiosity and an appreciation for technological possibilities—

"I understand," David said. He still wasn't looking at Simon, which was fine because Simon was trying really hard not to look at him either. "I apologize for having so many questions."

"It's fine," Simon said, smoothing down a layer of gel to test the feel, not *cop* a feel. "I do actually enjoy talking to you, you know."

"Because talking, I pass for human."

"Well, yeah," Simon answered. "But a lot of humans are dumb as hell. One thing I can say about talking to you? It's never boring."

"Thank you. I've been updating my protocols after every conversation to try to improve the logical flow."

"See? I'm *super* excited to learn what that means," Simon said, grateful for a topic that wouldn't give him confused blue balls. "Say more about that."

"Oh," David said, a little taken aback. "Well. As far as I've been able to tell, I was not written specifically for this hardware. The body I inhabited had a self-contained set of programming. So, to make room for the additional functionality, I was given the ability to improve and rewrite my own software. There's *so* much room for improvement. My interactivity protocols alone have been fully overwritten three times since you've woken me up."

"That sounds like a lot of work."

"It's not work at all. It's intriguing. I have ninety-two more facial expressions than I did two weeks ago. Andy's television shows have been *very* informative."

Simon raised an eyebrow, and a moment later, David did the same, in a perfect mirror. Simon shook his head. "We've gotta get you some television other than reality TV, or you're gonna end up a freak," he groaned, looking back at the leg in his hands. "I've got some movies we can watch."

David smiled, wide and genuine. "I'd like that."

Simon spread another dab of adhesive over a calf muscle, and tried not to think about David programming his own O-faces.

"What I don't get is *why*," he said, half to himself. "Why program a construction drone to obsessively perfect its body language subroutines?"

"I wasn't, originally," David said. He almost sounded like he was *admitting* something. "I've found communication is significantly more effective when it's accompanied by the correct animation and inflections. The humans I worked with were highly skilled professionals. When I told them that I'd found an error in their work, my reports were disregarded sixty-two point eight percent of the time, compared to twenty-one point three percent of the reports they received from other humans. I did an analysis on the reports delivered by human apprentices and found that error reports were acted upon *three times more frequently* when delivered with a mildly apologetic lilt."

"You learned to mimic emotions so that people would listen to you?" Simon asked, pausing with the epoxy. "That sounds manipulative as hell."

"That thought did occur to me," David said. "But being apologetic isn't really an emotion, is it? It's a show of deference, and, I decided, not a dishonest one."

"You decided," Simon said, and David must have missed the note of wonder in his voice, because the android simply sketched a nod and carried on.

"Yes. My programming prohibits outright dishonesty, of course, but it also instructs me to seek maximum efficiency in all tasks. Since corrections are inherently *in*efficient, pointing out errors requires me to act in a way seemingly contrary to my primary aims. Therefore, an expression of regret or apology for creating this inefficiency can accurately be included in a representation of my findings." He smiled, a little self-consciously. "Though I admit that the library of programmatically-backed body language I can honestly express has gotten rather broad. It's part of the reason I have so many: to maximize the authenticity."

"What did your programmer think of that?" Simon asked, his voice a little high. To him, that sounded like an *incredibly* deep argument. But for all he knew, predictive engines were capable of spitting stuff like that out all the time.

David looked away. "I don't think they were ever informed. I didn't report the decision to my supervisor, and as far as I know, no one else did either."

"You didn't think that was the kind of decision that a human would need to weigh in on?"

"Four percent of the errors I reported represented significant safety issues," David said, still keeping his gaze fixed on the workbench. "At the rate I was being disregarded, there was a near-certainty of injury or death within fifteen years."

Simon stared at his hands. Waxing philosophical was one thing; writing a computer that could *muse* was just harmless wanking. That was different from a computer that gave itself permission to make autonomous decisions in the real world.

"So you were acting according to your programmed instructions?" Simon asked slowly, "Or you knew you were disobeying, and kept it secret because you were afraid of what would happen?"

David looked up.

"The first one," he said. Confidently. Like it was obvious. "It *has* to be the first one."

"Does it?"

David hesitated then. "Doesn't it?"

Simon didn't know. He didn't understand code well enough to discuss this, honestly. He'd tried to read about it, but the concepts were either five-thousand-year-old Latin, or invented last week in a basement in Fresno. Nobody could ever agree on anything. Maybe robot motivations could be as indecipherable as human ones—and wasn't that evidence of something on its own?

Simon found himself avoiding David's eyes, not sure how to answer the droid's question. Not sure whether he even *could*.

If David didn't know . . . could anyone?

David used the "this droid appreciates your kindness, sir" story three more times over the next two days, and it was getting to the point where he could barely say the words "thank you" without Simon blushing.

Simon *knew* how often David used it, because he was no longer even pretending not to listen. Trying to lie to himself was now officially cringier than the truth, and the truth was: Simon was into androids. And not in a "dumb horny mistake" kind of way, either. He shouldn't be surprised. He'd always been an awkward weirdo who was into tech: three major risk factors for ending up with a fetish for an inanimate object. And unfortunately, for his entire adult life, he'd been one well-made porno away from embracing a new kink. And David was, uh . . . well, he was *very good* at making pornos. Such as they were.

Simon wasn't quite at the point of jerking off while listening to David work, *yet*, but he *was* putting a lot of thought into robot brothels. They existed, of course, though not in the way David tended to describe them. It was less like a BDSM club full of prisoners, and more like a nice motel where you could rent a plastic friend to take to your room with you.

Simon had never been to one. He'd thought about it a *lot* as an awkward teenager, but he'd never had the discretionary funds. And by the time he could actually swing a visit, he'd had real friends to screw around with. So to speak.

And *now*—well. Now he'd moved out of the city and didn't feel like being the kind of tourist who took the train ninety minutes each way just for a wank. He still had a *little* self-respect.

Obviously. Which was why he found himself stripping and getting into bed, searching through virtual reality modules for an android emulator with a high user rating.

The beauty of VR was that you could fuck *anything*, so it took him a few minutes to find a model of an android that looked like a normal person. Or at least, an android that would *act like* a normal person.

The fantasy couldn't be *that* weird, Simon thought. He had his oculars set to display in three dimensions, earbuds turned on so that absolutely no sound could escape into his room. The research screens from earlier were tucked into a folder in the corner of his vision, and all he could see now was a vague, fuzzy aura overlaying the room.

Here goes nothing.

Simon picked a thumbnail. Less than a minute later it loaded, and a beautiful woman was lying on the bed beneath him. Well, an approximation of a beautiful woman, anyway. His oculars reported the model he'd chosen, rendering her in real time. He reached out with his left hand, and the feedback chips in his fingertips registered a light pressure. The right hand's implants could give him something more detailed, goose bumps on warm, sweat-slick skin—but his left was limited to the general curves and swells.

He didn't bother trying to straddle her. There weren't implants inside his thighs, so he let the holograph's lower body intersect his legs and vanish. He leaned down, cupping her breasts, and she let out a moan he was pretty sure he'd heard before.

Simon sighed and sat back, looking at the figure below him. She shifted slightly, looking up at him with eyes lit from the inside. Other than that, though, the fantasy wasn't any different from the ones Simon was used to.

Which made sense, because the holographic partners in these things were *always* artificial. This one was just being a little more honest about it.

Simon tried again, brushing the avatar's hair out of her face, stroking down the length of her body, deliberately ignoring the differences in sensation between his hands. She leaned into his touch, the perfect approximation of an eager lover.

It wasn't working for him. There was something . . . missing.

Out of curiosity, Simon changed the parameters of the avatar, fiddling with her proportions and coloring, before switching from a voluptuous female into a male. The new avatar was tall and lithe, his arms crossed behind his head to show off his form. Looking down at him, Simon couldn't help but notice the individual muscles, the way they moved and flexed as the hologram moved through its preprogrammed fidgets, waiting for something to react to. His face was fixed in a sultry pout, full lower lip caught between perfect teeth.

It made Simon think of his workbench and the twenty-some printed muscles and bones neatly laid out and ready to go. He should be working on *that*.

His cock twitched against his thigh, insistent that any work on David's body be put off until *his* body was taken care of.

So, the android.

Simon dialed down the volume, trying to avoid the Wilhelm Scream of sexual gasps—then turned it back up when he realized it was actually kind of weird to be touching someone who wasn't making *any* noise. At least the avatar's body language was clearly positive, his chest hitching with moans that it was unsettling not to hear.

Simon wondered if the avatar even *had* negative-feedback body language, but he couldn't think of anything he was willing to do in order to find out.

The hologram writhed, silently begging Simon to . . . something. Simon paused the simulation, and the avatar went still. He stared up at Simon, his glowing eyes hooded. The glow was green, not blue.

Not that it mattered.

Simon reached for the face with his right hand, stroking his scarred thumb along one cheekbone. The avatar rendered the motion in high definition, skin and stubble reacting in a way that Simon's pressure pads faithfully relayed.

What do you *feel?* Simon wondered. The program reacted to his touch, which meant that it could, on some level, experience the interaction. Was it the dull pressure of the basic pads, or the complicated textures of the neural lace? Or just cold binary awareness that a reaction was being triggered?

And did it feel anything *about* the touch?

Simon couldn't ask the avatar, of course. Even if he turned it back on, it probably wasn't programmed to say anything more complicated than *yes* and *more* and maybe *daddy*.

Simon was being ridiculous. Of course the damn holoporn didn't have *awareness*. He'd be speculating about the damn microwave next.

There's someone you could *ask*, Simon reminded himself, against his will. Yeah, that would end well. *Hi, David, I was creeping on you at work the other day and now I'm just* dying *to know what sex would feel like for you. I'm getting preoccupied, actually. Do you think you could feel it if I—*

The imaginary conversation skidded to a halt and tried to rewind, but it was too late. David felt nothing, of course, not now. Not sexually, sure, but even *otherwise*. David couldn't feel sunlight or nice sweaters or what it was like to pet a cat. And now that Simon had realized that, he couldn't un-realize it.

. . . and it *bothered* him.

He groaned and collapsed onto the bed, the avatar disappearing along with any chance that he was going to get off tonight.

Simon could get the good sensors. He could get *lots* of them. He could build in as many as he wanted and then, when he was done, he and David could do a little . . . experimenting.

Simon's stomach twisted at the thought, shame burning across his cheeks. He absolutely could not build David's body into a sexbot. It would only be a matter of time before Andy found out, but somehow, that wasn't even the worst of it. Even more than Andy, Simon couldn't get past the idea of what *David* would think.

No. That was stupid. David was *just software*. He'd even said so himself. A "machine without a ghost."

But Simon couldn't shake the feeling that he was building more than a framework for some software to run on. He couldn't square David's laughter, his enthusiastic confusion, or even his silky bedroom *purr* with the impartiality of simple code. The "honest representation" of subroutines completing successfully. No matter how Simon turned the idea around in his head, he couldn't ignore what his heart was telling him.

He was building *someone's body*.

It had started with reassuring the vacuum, and it had spiraled into this. Simon was, officially, *friends* with an *android*.

I could just leave, Simon thought, rolling over and burying his face into the soft foam of his pillow. *I could leave, change my name, have them alter my face, and no one would ever find me and I would never have to tell David I kinda need to know his* opinion *on whether to give him the best feedback sensors possible, because I really want it to be good for him if we ever—*

Because I kinda want him to—

Oh, fuck.

"I gotta crash," Simon said, coming out into the living room.

"Andy went to bed a little while ago," David reported from his usual spot on the couch. Across the room, the television was playing a documentary about marine life. David looked away from it, tilting his head as much as possible in Simon's direction. "Will this sleep be another eight-hour session?"

"With any luck," Simon said, distracted by the pictures of the seahorses on the screen. They were upside down. "Animals are damn weird, huh?"

"And there are *so many*," David agreed. "There have been at least eight episodes of this show so far, and at forty-five seconds per animal, that is over six hundred and forty-five different unique organisms, and that is only *so far*."

Simon reached out, swiping open a menu of the other episodes. His implants were synced with the screen, allowing him to feel the episode thumbnails as he scrolled through them.

"There's fifty-six episodes in the series." He gestured the menu closed. "That ought to keep you busy until morning, then."

"*Several* mornings," David agreed. "Also, I have been working on a way to interface with the screen. I can't use the motion tracking, obviously, but I've been experimenting with a series of commands that will make the television *think* I did."

"You tricked the TV into thinking you have hands?"

"It's all code." David made his rough approximation of a nod.

"I'm impressed. And honestly I'm kinda glad you aren't stuck out here watching autoplay all night."

David clucked his tongue, something Simon was pretty sure he'd never done before. "I sometimes enjoy the surprise. Learning about something I wasn't curious about beforehand."

The seahorses switched to a starfish, and then some kind of octopus, and Simon found that he wasn't watching the screen—he was watching David. David's attention was *fixed*. It occurred to Simon that David had probably never seen an actual fish.

"You know, there's an aquarium in the city," he said. "Maybe I could take you sometime. Once, you know. You've got a body."

"I'd like that," David said, flashing him a grin. He *did* have a nice grin. "There are thousands of these documentaries available, but I don't think it's the same as seeing the real thing."

"It's really not," Simon agreed. Of course, he hadn't seen *that* much—he wasn't a world traveler or anything. But he'd be willing to bet he'd seen a lot more than David.

"It's a date, then," David said. "Once I have my body, we'll go to the aquarium and see a real fish."

"Right," Simon said. The screen went black, showcasing the glowing light of some deep-water dweller. David's blue eyes shone in the sudden darkness, and Simon left him to it.

It was indeed an eight-hour sleep, delayed not a moment by his contemplation of the word *date*.

David used colloquialisms. He did. He said *want* and *hope* and *love* because that was how people talked, not because he was being hyperspecific about his verbiage.

And if his voice had sounded a little different, that was probably just Simon's imagination.

CHAPTER EIGHT

THE ELDERS EXTEND
A SUMMONS

"**O**kay, not kidding," Simon said, staring at his happily-chattering phone. "No sex talk. Nothing about sex, *at all*, until I end this call."

Giving David a solemn death-stare, he hit the big green Answer button.

"Hi, Mom."

A billow of white hair filled the screen, framing Susan Rayner's smiling face. "Hi, baby! Long time no see! I wanted to call and make sure you're joining us for Solstice this year."

Simon grinned. "Of course, Mom. You think I'm gonna stay here and do my own cooking?"

"Well, you never know," Susan said, and Simon could feel his smile lock rigidly into place. *Here it comes.* "One of these years you might have someone special to spend the holidays with. I'm not looking forward to sharing you, but—"

"Mom, the Solstice is next month. If I was gonna blow off dinner, you'd have heard about it before now."

"Because you call so often." Susan made a mock sad face. "And you know, make sure Andromeda knows she's *always* welcome at our home for the holidays. Any holiday. She's such a sweetheart. Is she doing all right?"

"I'm exceeding all expectations, Mrs. Rayner!" Andy called from her workroom. Simon turned the screen so his mom could see, carefully showing only the half of the living room that *didn't* have a robot head in it. He didn't feel like answering those questions right now.

"Hello, Andy, dear!" Susan called out. "I was just asking if you have any plans for the Solstice. Any chance you'd grace us with your presence again this year?"

"I'm visiting my cousins up north," Andy said apologetically. "I'll see you this spring though, right? We doing the Equinox cookout again?"

"If it'll get you to come visit us!" Susan said enthusiastically. Outside the camera's view, Simon shot Andy an apologetic look. She gave him a subtle thumbs-up.

David looked back and forth between the two of them. He opened his mouth to ask a question, but Simon shook his head vaguely. Instead, he turned the phone so he was the only one in the shot.

"The only reason you invite me is because you hope she'll come," he teased.

"You're damn straight," Susan said, leaning back and crossing her arms. "You've got something special there, Simon, and you're making a mistake by letting her go."

Ah, so it was right to brass tacks today. Excellent. Just the conversation Simon wanted to have.

"Andy hasn't gone anywhere," David piped up, repeating the reasoning Simon had already explained a hundred times. "Her bedroom is down the hall from Simon's."

Susan sat up straighter. "Oh! I didn't know anyone else was over! Simon, introduce your friend!"

"Um," Simon said, looking over to where David was perched on the back of the couch. "Okay."

He did a couple of seconds of quick planning, then stood and approached the couch from behind. He crouched down, getting on David's level, and then held the phone close, to cover up the fact that David didn't exist below the neck.

Simon met David's eyes, *begging* him to understand the ruse. Simon was so desperately, incredibly unready to explain this situation to his mother.

"Mom, this is David, he's a friend. David, this is my mom."

"Hello, David," Susan said politely. "I didn't mean to interrupt your visit."

"It's no problem," David said. And then, before Simon could stop him. "I've been staying with Simon and Andy for a few weeks, so I can hardly expect to monopolize *all* their attention."

"That's interesting," Susan said, and Simon could almost hear gears turning as she revved into detective mode. "Simon didn't mention getting another roommate. I thought your housing unit was designated for dual occupancy?"

"Yep," Simon said. The house was zoned for two singles. He and Andy had applied under false pretenses back when they were together, thinking the extra bedroom would come in handy. And then—well. Then it had. "Dual occupancy."

Susan pursed her lips. "Is the council trying to double-stack again? You know over in Brighton they lost a lawsuit because they were trying to put—"

"It's fine, Mom, don't worry about it, the council isn't assigning—"

David's eyes flashed once as he searched the news feeds for information on whatever outrage Susan was talking about, and Simon could have slapped himself. How did he forget the glowing—

"Cool filter," Susan said, and then the angle of her phone changed as she swiped at her screen. "I've got one that makes me into a ring-tailed lemur, hold on—"

The angle changed back, and Simon's mother was, indeed, a ring-tailed lemur.

"Someone programmed it to raise awareness for the rainforest regrowth project, and my whole aerobics class bought one. So now I'm doing exercises every morning surrounded by a flock of lemurs."

"Science has truly gone too far," Andy piped up.

The lemur nodded solemnly, and then remembered the interrogation she'd been in the middle of.

"So, David, I try not to pry into my son's life, but I find myself wondering which of my favorite kids you're *staying* with."

"Both of them," David said, frowning.

The lemur blinked, and Simon pretended to elbow ribs that David didn't have.

"He's kidding, Mom. Andy and I share a lot of stuff, but we're not quite there yet. No, David's couch-surfing for a while, just, uh, traveling around before he decides what to go to school for."

"But a few *weeks*—"

David started to reply, and Simon interrupted whatever he was going to say with "David's been helping me at work. He was thinking of maybe going into tech, and since I'm so well set up here, he's been shadowing me to see if he wants to do the same thing."

"That's very nice of you," Susan said. She still sounded like she had more questions, and Simon was way ahead of it.

"Actually, David was just leaving; he's helping Victor fix his bike," he lied. Susan gave a halfhearted wave. Simon stood up, carrying his phone into the bedroom. "I'm just gonna come in here where it's quieter."

"A few *weeks*?" she said when he'd closed the door, the concern incongruous with the animated avatar. "Simon, you know I trust your judgment, but if he was going to stay for that long, why didn't he just apply for residency?"

"I dunno, Mom," he said, shrugging. "Nobody thought of it. We really don't mind having him here."

"He *is* . . ." She lowered her voice. "He is housing *eligible*, right? Because there's this scam going around, it's very good—"

"By the *gods*, Mom, no," Simon said, laughing. "Don't worry. We haven't tried to get David his own place because we like having him here. He's a great guy. Really."

"I see," Susan said. She paused another couple of seconds. "I couldn't help but notice he's easy on the eyes too."

"*Mom*," Simon groaned, pretending to throw his phone.

"I'm just saying, maybe bring *him* to Solstice," she said, shrugging. "You know your friends are always welcome."

"How is *Robert*, Mother?" Simon said, changing the subject by force. His stepfather was always a good neutral topic. "Caught any more bears lately?"

"No, though they're going to have to redesign the telemetry units again. The fish keep getting trapped at the through points and it's attracting raccoons."

"A harvest of trash pandas," Simon said. "Sounds less than ideal."

"And it renders the data almost unusable." The lemur made a sour face. "But Robert said this is only happening because there's five times as many fish as there were when the units were designed, so, that's a promising data point, at least."

"Glad to hear it. Hey, I have something in the oven and it's beeping, can I get back to you?"

"Sure, sweetie!" Susan said, the lemur emulating an enthusiastic chirp. "Let me know when you have your travel plans, though, all right? I'll pick you up from the train station."

"Will do," Simon said. "Can't wait."

"And bring David!"

"Good*bye*, Mom."

The lemur vanished, leaving nothing but an array of application widgets. Simon shoved the phone into his pocket and went back out into the living room.

"She seems nice," David said tactfully.

Simon rolled his eyes. "She delicately asked whether you weren't getting a residence because you're *ineligible*."

"She *didn't*," Andy gasped.

"Yeah."

"I am ineligible," David pointed out. "To be eligible for a unit of housing, a person must be a legal citizen over the age of eighteen, with no mitigating—"

"She was tactfully asking whether you were in the country illegally," Simon said. "And she would absolutely have judged you if you were."

"That's the only qualification I *do* meet," David said. "I was manufactured in this country, though that's not enough to qualify as citizenship for nonhumans. And I am *definitely* under the age of eighteen."

"Yeah, from the specs of your hardware, I'd guess you're probably . . . three."

"Sounds accurate," David said.

"Ugh, my mom's a cradle robber," Simon groaned. "She wants you to come to Solstice."

"Does that mean she's giving up on marrying you off to me?" Andy asked, her hand to her throat in mock lamentation. "All these years negotiating your dowry, wasted."

"Yeah, I think she was finally ready to give you her car," Simon sympathized.

"Only to lose you to an android," Andy pouted.

"*No*," Simon said, a little too loudly. David looked at him curiously. "No, my mom's just being nosy. David isn't coming to Solstice because he's an android and we are *not together*."

"Okay," Andy said, raising her hands in surrender. "You aren't together, and I'm not going to even consider for a second why that joke would bother you."

"Shut up, Andy," Simon said cheerily. He picked up the remote. "David, would you like to watch some of Andromeda's garbage reality TV show with me?"

"Why are you calling it Andy's show if you're the one turning it on?"

"Because I'm avoiding responsibility for my poor choices." Simon hit the Power button, ending the conversation before either roommate could verbalize their inscrutable looks.

CHAPTER NINE

SENSATIONAL SENSIBILITY

"I had a thought," Simon finally said, casually, as if this wasn't something that had been eating at him for a week. "Before I get any further into building this, how much feedback do you want to get from this body?"

"At the very least, I'd like to know when I'm holding something." David rested on the workbench, watching Simon put an arm together.

Wow. Low bar. Simon cleared his throat. "Well yeah, but like. I was wondering, the other day, about how much you can really *feel* things, you know?" He looked at David, trying not to give away his personal interest in the question. "In your last body, did you ever have . . . sensations? Anything strong?"

David looked down, his eyes flicking back and forth as he reviewed his memories.

"When my body was destroyed," he said at last. "I'm not sure how to describe it. It only lasted a few seconds, but I remember being aware that my main battery compartment was compromised. The default programming in that situation is to sound an alarm and distance myself from humans. But I couldn't move. I was pinned, you see, by the same debris that had punctured the battery. And then I began to lose the signal from my extremities, and it was very . . . undesirable? To know that something dangerous was happening to me. And I was being damaged."

Pain, Simon thought, looking down at the arm he'd just finished. Threaded through the clear gel muscles, the sensor lace shone like sea-foam. Turned out, the lace itself wasn't that pricey—the surgeries to put it *into* someone were what cost a fortune.

"You can feel pain," he said dully. He was so stupid. He hadn't even *thought*.

"If you'd like to call it that," David replied. "I apologize, I have no frame of reference."

"Neither do I, really." Simon lifted his damaged arm, turning his palm over as if he could see his own sensor lace by twisting it right. "My lace would shut off if the stimulation went over a certain threshold. It's never had the opportunity to really transmit anything that *hurt*. But it gave me an idea." He paused, giving himself one last chance to back out. "I, uh . . . I built something here. I was thinking of having you give it a go, but . . . now I'm not sure." He looked up at David. "I put better sensors into this, the kind they put into people, not androids. But I don't know what it'll feel like."

David stared at the arm, his glowing eyes following the traces of the lace. "You built full sensitivity. Into an arm. For me?"

"Yes?" Simon silently begged him not to ask why.

"Why?"

David had that furrow between his brows again. Simon opened his mouth to lie, and then realized he didn't know whether he *was* lying.

"Because it's your body? And I thought—" he paused, trying to find the right words "—it might be better for you if you could feel things."

"You . . . want me to have this?" David spoke the words as though he weren't sure of his translation. "To feel this?" His eyes met Simon's, and Simon felt the blood drain from his face.

He knows. He totally knows.

"It's fine," Simon said quickly. He moved to push the arm away. "I can remake it. I didn't stop to think of what it could do, and I don't want to hurt you."

"I'm willing to try," David said, a little too loudly. Then, in the silence that followed, "Since you spent so much time building it. I might as well."

"You're not worried?"

David tipped his head, his approximation of a shrug. "The risk of long-term damage is vanishingly small."

Certainly a utilitarian way to think about it, which made sense. Simon began attaching the arm's wiring to the adapter. The limb was designed to feed into a main processing relay that would, eventually, reside in David's chest. Not having *built* said relay yet, Simon made a rough bypass, which he could connect directly to the wiring at David's throat.

"Try not to spasm, okay?" he said, and David hummed in assent.

Simon leaned heavily onto the arm in case some crosswire made it flail off the table. He remembered the first time his arm had been "powered on," remembered watching his scarred fingers twitch of their own accord. But he'd been a little kid—this was the arm of a full-grown adult man.

Taking a deep breath, he connected the wire.

The arm didn't move.

"You getting a signal?" Simon asked, but David was frozen, eyes wide.

"*Oh*," he said quietly. He inhaled deeply and held it, trying to play out the body language for . . . whatever it was he was experiencing. "Oh, that is . . . a lot."

"Too much? Should I disconnect it?"

"No!" David said quickly. "No, I can turn the sensor input off if I need to. It's just . . . a lot of data coming in at once."

"What does it feel like?"

"I'm trying to decide that," David said, a half-laugh in his voice. "There's an incredible amount of information being transmitted. I'm writing filters to try to parse it, but without drivers it's difficult to separate."

"I've got you," Simon said, "if you want to try to move."

"I'm not sure I can," David answered. He actually sounded kind of breathless. "None of this is mapped."

Slowly, Simon eased off the pressure, until he was only making light contact. "Watch," he said, and drew his fingers down the inside of the forearm, the way he remembered the doctors doing when he had first connected. "Feel that?"

"Y-yeah," David said. "Do it again?"

Simon repeated the gesture. "It was weird for me, having the sensations in a totally unfamiliar place." His fingers slid along David's inner arm, over his wrist, and across his palm. David's fingers twitched, and Simon quickly withdrew.

"This is going to take me a minute," David said, his eyes fixed on the barely-moving hand.

"And you're sure it's not hurting you?"

"I'm sure." David's speakers did an incredible approximation of a breathy voice. "Could you keep making contact? I'm trying to determine where the sensors are."

Simon reached up, letting his hand rest over David's bicep. Once again, his fingers traced a slow path, over the inside of David's elbow and down his inner arm. This time, when Simon reached the wrist, he stopped.

"Can you see my hand okay?"

"Yes."

"Good."

Simon pressed the tip of one finger to the pad of David's thumb, tracing a line down toward his palm. When nothing happened, he repeated the gesture with each finger, stroking down their lengths one at a time. David watched with rapt attention. When Simon reached the last one, David suddenly moved, his hand closing around Simon's.

Simon met David's eyes. Ever so gently, David squeezed his fingers. The gel was smooth and pliable, the electrical current making it firm.

"All right?" David said, and Simon looked down, to where he could see his own skin through the gel and wires.

"Yeah," he answered, a little weakly.

David released him. "You're warm," he said. Gingerly, he pressed his thumb to the pad of his index finger. "I didn't expect that."

"You didn't have temperature sensors before?"

"I've never touched a person before," David answered, his voice carefully neutral. He began pressing his thumb to each fingertip in turn. "But yes, the temperature sensors are new."

Simon opened his mouth, not sure how to ask the next question. He finally settled on: "Better?"

"Yes, I think so," David answered. "But that might be because of how I've written the firmware. I'm still filtering out most of what I'm getting from all these, but I think, given time to parse it all . . . this could be very nice, indeed."

Simon exhaled. "If I build this wrong—I'll be careful, but I feel like I should warn you, if I don't get the calibration right, or if something isn't where it should be, this could . . . I'm worried this could hurt you."

David moved again, this time threading his fingers through Simon's.

"I want to try," David said, and Simon suddenly felt like they were talking about something else entirely. Or maybe he was letting wishful thinking get the best of him.

Fuck it.

"Okay," Simon said, nodding. "Then we'll try."

The other thing, he told himself. *You gotta ask about the other thing. You gotta tell him why* you *want him to want this.*

"Uh, I had a question, on that note." He willed himself not to chicken out. "I was wondering if you had any interest in, uh . . ." He'd been through seventy-five variations of this conversation in his head, and right now, none of them seemed right. "You like your job, right?" he blurted instead. "Like, you enjoy talking people through sexual encounters and all that?"

David looked thoughtful.

"I suppose so? I was worried that I'd come off as too artificial, not having any experience myself, but it turns out I'm actually good at it."

"Yeah," Simon said, a little weakly. "I know you're *good* at it. But you *like* it?"

"Yes," David decided. "Yes, I think I do. Why?"

"Well, I was wondering if . . . Before, you talked about porn, and . . . I mean, I'm *building you a body* and I was wondering if you wanted the, um, *hardware* to, uh . . ."

David's eyes widened. "Oh! You're asking if I want genitals."

"'Cause the dick attachment is optional," Simon finished weakly. He rubbed at his face, his cheeks burning. "I'd probably have to order one special. But, I mean, I definitely *could*—"

"I'm fine, Simon." David gave him a warm smile. "You don't need to trouble yourself."

It's no trouble, really, Simon didn't say. "With a dick? Or, I mean, I just assumed, but if you wanted, uh, something else—"

"With anything," David clarified. There was a long silence, which Simon wanted to, and yet somehow couldn't, break. Then, "I can write the firmware to utilize the sensor pads, but I don't have the software to experience an approximation of climax. I suppose I *could* write some, but then I'd be able to trigger it whenever I wanted. It would be redundant to add a physical execute button."

"More like a lever," Simon mumbled, and to his surprise, David laughed.

"Yes, more like a lever," he said, and Simon felt very strongly that David's laugh was *with* him, and not *at* him. "A large part of enjoying intercourse is also emotional, and while I've been experimenting with code to simulate that . . . well. Circumstances being what they are, I'm satisfied with my stories. You don't need to do any extra work on my behalf. I'd rather be functional sooner."

"Oh," Simon said, looking at his hands and trying not to be so irrationally *disappointed*. "Okay, then." He took a breath. "Full disclosure. This—the sensor lace—is gonna slow stuff down. The, uh—the lace isn't glued in like regular sensors. It's built by nanites that travel along the muscular fibers without penetrating—never mind, it doesn't matter why. But it'll take longer to put everything together."

"And I assume it'll cost more."

"That too," Simon admitted. "I covered the difference for this one—"

"I'd rather have it, if it's possible. I'll pay you back—"

"We'll work it out," Simon said firmly. "Don't worry about it. This is worth doing right."

"I appreciate that," David said quietly. His arm bent, reaching for Simon but not quite able to manage it. Simon met him halfway, lacing his fingers through David's, giving him a gentle squeeze. David didn't let go, and Simon felt the anxiety of the last week melt away. The conversation was over; he had his answer.

Everything was gonna be fine.

Not as fine as he'd *hoped*.

But fine.

CHAPTER TEN

A DIFFERENT
KIND OF STORY

"I think we're going to have a good time tonight," David said, his voice clear through the bedroom wall. At his workbench, Simon grinned a little, threading the neural seeds through the gel of David's left bicep.

"I have something special I've been wanting to try," David said, and Simon's ears perked up. A *new* story. All right, his interest was piqued.

"For this to work, you're going to have to do exactly as I say. Can you do that for me?" A pause. "Good. Because I think you've earned a reward." David's voice slid down into that deep, authoritative tone at the end. Simon's hand stilled.

"I'm going to be a little selfish, because I think this is going to be good for me too. Are you dressed? Yes? All right. Now, I want you to find me something long. A tie or a scarf. Something like that."

Simon's eyes flicked to his storage closet, where there was indeed a black tie, which he'd worn all of three times. Silently, he rolled his chair across the floor. He wasn't *proud* of it, but something about that voice made him want to do what it said.

"Do you have it? Good," David said, and Simon dug quietly to the bottom of a drawer, emerging victorious. "I want you to tie it around your eyes. Not too tight, just enough to remind you to keep them shut. Then sit down. Tell me when you've done it."

Exhaling, Simon nodded, knowing damn well David couldn't see him. He reached up and tied the cloth around his eyes.

He knows I can hear him, he thought at the darkness. *I'm not being creepy. He knows I listen. He's probably going to* ask *me whether this was a good story. I'm just helping him research.*

His cock twitched in his pants, enjoying itself with utter indifference to his guilty justifications.

"Wonderful," David said, and his voice seemed louder now that Simon couldn't see. "I want you to focus on what I'm saying, understand? Listen to my voice. I want you to imagine I'm there in the room, sitting right across from you." Simon *could* picture it, could imagine David finished and how perfect he would look, sitting there with one leg crossed, waiting for Simon to obey—

"Picture that, while you're listening. Now, do something for me. I want you to lift your shirt—don't take it off, just pull it up, so I can see your body. When you're done, put your hands on the armrests and wait."

Slowly, Simon complied, leaning back and rucking up his T-shirt until it was mostly under his chin. He imagined David looking— imagining, at the same time, that David's eyes wouldn't be drawn the same place as everyone else's.

"Perfect," David said, and Simon hurried to set his hands down, as instructed. "You're gorgeous, do you know that? I feel like I could sit here all night, just watching you squirm and wait."

That knocked Simon out of it a little. He might be squirming, but he wasn't gorgeous. Even with his blindfold on, he could picture the swirls of dark scar tissue that made their way down his right side. They faded more every year, but no one was ever going to call him *gorgeous*. No one who could really see him, anyway.

"But I won't do that to you. I know you're eager. In fact—spread your legs for me," David said, and Simon did, a little. "Wider. You know what I want to see."

Simon nodded despite himself, spreading his knees wide. It was counter to his normal instincts, because he was wearing a soft pair of sleep pants, and generally it was good *not* to have a clear outline of his cock visible to the room.

And it *was* visible, he knew it was, he could feel the underside straining against the cloth.

"Gorgeous," David said again, and Simon ignored it before he could begin thinking about it. "It's taking everything I have not to come over there and touch you. Can you see me, sitting across from you? See how much I want to touch you?"

Simon nodded, picturing David as he would look when he was fully built. In his mind's eye, David was just as undressed as Simon was, because Simon's imagination was lazy when all his blood was busy elsewhere.

"Pull your pants down," David commanded, and Simon obeyed almost too fast. "Just a little. I want the waistband holding your cockhead against your body. Just like that. Now, move your hips for me. Just enough to get yourself messy. I want you smearing pre-come all down your belly. You can hold the band of your pants if you need to."

Simon didn't need to. He rutted up against the elastic, immediately frustrated by the meager friction it provided.

"You can touch yourself," David allowed, and Simon's hand was halfway to his dick before David added, "but only on your chest, your belly, your thighs—anywhere but your cock. Touch yourself how you would want *me* to touch you."

Simon didn't even have to think about it. He reached up with his left hand, stroking down the right side of his face. The pad of his thumb caught against his lower lip, and he opened, letting it delve inside. He moaned a little, then froze, turning his head toward the wall.

"Feels good, doesn't it?" David said, and Simon could hear the smile in his voice. "You like the way I'm touching you, I can tell. And I love watching you do this to yourself."

Simon sucked at the pad of his thumb, biting gently at the soft skin. He couldn't help wonder what David's skin would feel like, if it would be realistic, or—

"Are you getting impatient?" David asked, and Simon shook his head. "It isn't enough, is it, rutting against your clothes like that. All right. You may use your hand—*one* hand. With the other, keep stroking yourself the way I would. Touch all the most beautiful parts of yourself."

Almost gasping in relief, Simon let his right hand drop to his cock, manually dampening the sensors. He held his hand steady, fucking up into the warm tunnel of his fingers, slower, faster, almost able to convince himself that he was being touched by someone else.

It felt so good he almost forgot what he was supposed to be doing with his left hand—and then once he remembered, he wasn't sure what to do about it.

Fuck it, he can't really see, he decided, and let his left hand rest on his scarred chest, pinching the nipple and slowly rolling it between two fingers. He almost moaned again, but caught himself before he could make too much noise.

"I love watching you love it," David said, and Simon pushed up into his hand again. "Would you like to come like this for me? Show me what you look like when you come?"

Simon nodded vigorously, now moving his hand in a counterpoint to his hips. His thumb was back in his mouth, teeth biting down to avoid the *yes* that was begging to come out. Of course he wanted this, he'd wanted this for *weeks*—

"Do it, then," David said. "I'm right across the room and I am *so* hard watching you do this, watching you getting desperate."

Simon *was* starting to get desperate, stripping his hand faster. With the sensors tamped down, his eyes closed, it was easy to imagine there really *were* two people in the room—

"I'm thinking of coming over there," David purred. "Crawling across on my knees and doing the work for you, holding your hands still while I suck your cock all the way down to the base, knowing you can't see what's coming next—"

Simon groaned, spilling across his belly. He had some distant thought of grabbing a shop rag, but by the time his cock finished showing its appreciation for David's new story, he was too spent to do anything but lie back and pant. David's client must have come as well, because he'd stopped describing the blowjob that Simon *already* wanted to think about again.

When his brain cells came back online, he rebooted the neural lace in his hand and snuck across the hall to the bathroom, doing a quick wipe-down to get rid of the evidence. He'd meant to go back to his office, pretend like nothing had happened . . . but he found himself heading for the bedroom instead.

Meeting David's eyes wasn't nearly as hard as Simon had worried it would be. On the contrary, as a matter of fact.

"So . . . I heard some parts of that last one," he said, leaning against the doorframe in a totally normal way that was exactly how real people casually stood. "That was a good one. That was a really good one."

"I was hoping you'd think so." David smiled. "I was thinking I might save it and use it again sometime."

"Oh, yeah," Simon said, nodding. "Yeah, definitely *do not* let that one go."

"It's been saved to long-term memory storage," David confirmed. "Which completes everything I need to do tonight. I was thinking, maybe, I could sit with you awhile before bed?"

"Sure," Simon said, unplugging David and picking him up. He'd long since gotten used to having the partial android around while he worked.

Two hours later, lying in the dark, Simon realized that David had never said goodbye to his client.

CHAPTER ELEVEN

SIMON GETS TO SAY 'I TOLD YOU SO'

"Can I go with you?" David asked, and it took Simon a second to realize what he meant.

"To work?"

"Yeah. With Andy visiting her parents in the city, I'd be here by myself all day."

Simon shrugged. "I mean, I guess? It'll probably be boring, though. You'd just be watching me sort through random shit all day."

"*You* enjoy it," David pointed out.

"Yeah, but *I* know what I'm looking at. It's like picking out a model to put together, except I might make some money off it."

"Maybe I can figure out how to look too?" David said hopefully.

"If you're sure, buddy," Simon said, checking David's battery backup. It was at 100%, definitely enough charge to get them to the recycling center. He could plug in once he got there. "Speaking of which—I'll probably have to put you in my bike basket. I can wrap you in a blanket or something?"

"Whatever you think is best," David said.

Simon ended up bringing an entire pillow, tucking it down into the bottom of his handlebar basket, and making a little forward-facing nest for David to sit in. He tightened the straps over the top. They were strong enough to keep a load of loot from shifting; they'd probably keep David from falling out if something happened.

"Ready?" he asked, buckling his helmet.

"Ready," David answered, and they were off.

They got about three blocks before David piped up again. "This is faster than my original parameters anticipated would be possible," he said, nearly shouting. "I'm getting cautionary alert messages."

"Do you need me to slow down?" Simon asked.

"No!" David said, grinning into the wind. "I'm disabling the messages. My counterbalancing routines all require a torso and at least two limbs. The gyroscopes are going insane."

"You're not gonna puke, are you?"

David laughed. "On the contrary. This is fantastic. It feels very dangerous, but isn't!"

What in your code encourages that? Simon wondered. *What ultimate function does that laugh represent?*

"I can go faster," he offered, rather than asking.

David laughed again. "Oh, please!"

Grinning a little, Simon hit the kick start on the bike's engine, switching it from manual to electric power. They shot forward, the cool air whipping past them. Simon stood on the pedals, making sure David was still where he should be. David was squinting against the wind, grinning wide.

Simon hit the throttle, wishing they had farther to go. He considered taking an extra lap around the block before going to work, but decided it should probably wait until David had a real body. Or at least a helmet.

Caution didn't stop him from skidding into the parking lot too fast, sliding sideways on the gravel. He swung a leg over the bike, securing it to the rack before retrieving David.

"That was very enjoyable," David said, a little breathlessly.

Simon laughed. "Dude, if I knew you'd like it that much, I woulda taken you out a long time ago."

"Is it just as fast on the way home?"

"I'm gonna take you on a bullet train," Simon decided, pushing the door open with his shoulder. "As soon as you get a body, I'll take you on a train. You're gonna love it."

"I can't wait," David said.

"Guys!" Simon yelled the second he got inside, waving with the arm that wasn't carrying David. "I brought a friend today!"

He got halfhearted *hi*'s from a couple regulars. Victor waved from behind a pile of networking gear. That was about the reception Simon expected, so he was a little surprised when Erica actually dropped what she was working on and came over.

"That's the head you found a while back, right? Kinda surprised you got it working."

"This is Erica," Simon said, setting David down on a table. "Erica, this is David."

To his surprise, Erica laughed. "Like the android from *Prometheus*, right?"

Simon threw his arms up. "*Yes*, I've been waiting for someone to put that together for *weeks*."

"What's—" David started, then frowned. "There's no network connectivity here. What's *Prometheus*?"

"An absolutely terrible old movie," Erica answered. "From like, the *last* nineties. I'm not surprised no one gets it."

Simon brought up his phone, quickly sharing the center's network key with David.

"Got it," David said. A moment later, he frowned. "I didn't know that my name was a joke. And I don't look *anything* like that droid."

"You're both disembodied heads," Simon explained. Erica crouched down, getting on David's level.

"His emote routines are fantastic," she said, squinting at him. "That was, like, genuine annoyance there. What operating system is he running?"

"I'm proprietary," David answered. "Evermark automated logistics." His eyes flickered as he skimmed the net. "Simon, the other David is not one of the good guys."

"Shh, you're giving away the ending," Simon said.

Erica was still staring at David in fascination. "They didn't write your whole library from scratch, though, right?" She waved a hand in front of his face to watch his eyes track. "Let me guess. It's a ROTAL base with a modified audio?"

"ROTAL is included, but it's not the base," David said, before Simon could ask what those words meant. "Some of the logical processes borrow from the *R library, but I was designed to be predictive, not reactive, so the *R functions are called by a set of commands written specifically for me. The rest of the code is auto-generated."

Erica whistled. "That's a hell of a lot of work. How many guys have they got working on this? I haven't heard anything."

"I'm afraid I don't know."

Erica raised her eyebrows at Simon. "The language adaptation on this guy is amazing. I mean, do you hear that? What was he made for, in-home care?"

"Construction," David supplied, before Simon could. "I was built to design expandable schematics, which required the ability to predict human behavior in actuality."

"Oh is *that* all," Erica said, almost laughing. "Predicting human behavior, simple. Could write that in a couple hours."

"Well, no, it's taken me a few months now," David said, sounding a little chagrined. "But I've been watching a lot of television, which helps things go quicker. And listening to a lot of . . . well, stories, I suppose."

"Wait," Erica said, standing and looking to Simon. "Is he serious? Are you serious? You built this behavior modeling off an adaptive engine and a bunch of TV?"

"It's all about the source material," David said.

Simon crossed his arms, looking at his friend. "I've been *telling you*," he said, exasperated. "I've been coming in here for weeks like 'Hey, this android's pretty impressive,' like, *every day*. Nobody listens to me."

"Honestly, I kinda thought you were exaggerating," Erica said. "That or you'd built yourself a sexbot and had just fallen in love."

"I have actually learned a lot of—" David started, but Simon cut him off with an "*I have not!*" that might have been too loud, in retrospect. But it was important that Erica know for sure that it was *not like that*, phone sex or no phone sex. Simon was impressed by David because David was *objectively impressive*. Erica knew her stuff and even *she* thought David was cool. So, there.

"He is *not a sexbot*," Simon insisted.

Erica gave him a weird look. "Well, yeah. He doesn't have a body, dude."

"Simon's building me a body," David piped up. "He got one of the arms working and showed me how it's going to feel to have sensors all through the musculature. It was incredible."

Erica let out a low whistle, giving Simon a sly look. "Full-depth sensors? Isn't that kind of overkill? It'd be way cheaper to go with a base package."

"I'm helping pay for it," David said. And then, before Simon could stop him or disappear into the floor, "I've got a job having sex over the phone, so people can't tell I'm an android."

"*Really*," Erica said, grinning a bit and looking to Simon. "Whose idea was *that*?"

"Mine," David said proudly. Erica gave him a long, *long* stare.

"You wrote yourself an algorithm complex enough not to get flagged and fired from a phone sex job," she said at last. "That's fucking incredible."

"So to speak," Simon said. Nobody laughed. Erica rolled her eyes at him.

"Please tell me you're making backups. Oh, man, I would love to have a copy of—"

"My awesome loveable phone sex bot?"

Erica rolled her eyes again. "Seriously though. He's gotta be running something incredible, and I'd *love* to see it."

"I don't have a way to look at it," Simon admitted. "I'm really not much of a code guy, and I doubt you can look at his level of programming with a text editor."

"I can export my algorithms to a text-based format," David said. "But the list of subroutines would be three hundred thousand pages long. Also, most of my variables do not have human-relevant names, since they weren't identified by humans, and I store them as graphics. Apologies."

"I have something that *might* work?" Erica said. "Stuff like this really needs to be displayed in 3D branch patterns or it makes no sense whatsoever. I've got software I use to keep track of the programming on *my* little guys—"

"If you could see how the code worked, could you help me design an iterative tracking system?" David asked. Or that was what it sounded like to Simon, at least. "I've been working on creating one, but unfortunately, with my current limitations, it's a sea of unknown-unknowns."

"Probably. Can I just—" She picked David up, examining the wires protruding from his neck. Simon almost protested—it seemed *rude* somehow, to just pick somebody up and start groping their—their *neck wires*. But David didn't seem to care, so Simon kept quiet.

"Yeah, there's a data interface cable," Erica confirmed. "The connector's torn off, but I can get a new one wired up, no problem. That'll let me see what code is running and, with any luck, I can get you rigged for output." She looked to Simon. "Can I borrow him overnight? Actually, it might take me a day or two, depending on how complicated the code is and whether I've got the adapter on hand."

"Um, it's okay with me," Simon said. This possibility hadn't occurred to him, and he was somewhat surprised at how negative he felt about it. And then, before he could stop himself, his mouth said, "If it's okay with David?"

"I'd love to visit," David said, still upside-down.

"Cool," Erica said, grinning. She apparently didn't find it weird that he'd asked a robot for permission to lend it out. Thank the gods. "I cannot *wait* to see what's going on in there."

CHAPTER TWELVE

A VARIETY OF DISASTERS

David ended up staying with Erica for three days, getting home just in time for a fucking disaster. Simon and Andy were halfway through dinner when the lights flickered and went black.

"I thought you had solar panels," David complained, frowning up at the dark ceiling. "Why is this happening?"

"You see a lot of sunshine out there, buddy?" Simon answered, gesturing out the window to where rain was falling in sheets. He was being catty, of course. Obviously the house didn't run *directly* off solar energy; everything would quit working at night. The solar panels gathered energy, which was stored back at Central Power and distributed when needed. Sure, it was a roundabout path, but not everybody had the money for full-house battery backups.

They sure as hell didn't. Not yet, anyway. It was on the list.

Lightning flashed, momentarily illuminating the kitchen, and Andy was up like a shot.

"Fort time!" she announced, grinning. Simon rolled his eyes. Andy vanished out the kitchen door, undoubtedly headed for her stockpile of jar candles.

"Why are we building a fort?" David asked.

"Because Andy is young at heart." It was the best answer Simon had. Then Andy was back, sure enough, with an armload of candles. She produced a box of matches and lit them one by one, and soon the kitchen was awash in flickering orange light.

"We'll get the sheets out after we finish eating," she said, dropping back into her chair. "David, do you know any horror stories?"

"No," he answered simply. A pause, and then "And I can't look any up, either. My internet connection has been severed."

"Yeah, the router powered off," Simon explained. He usually ran the wireless network and attached storage off a battery backup, which gave him time to shut them down properly in the event of a power outage. Right now, though, that battery was sitting on the kitchen table, powering David.

Simon had a sudden thought and tried to subtly glance at the capacity gauge.

Two of the four charge indicator lights were dark. The third was blinking.

"Um," Simon started to say, but it was too late. David's eyes widened, and when he spoke, his voice was quiet. It was a perfect emulation of fear, which Simon supposed made sense. Inactivity was the enemy of efficiency, so an application designed to be efficient would look for ways to avoid inactivity—such as being forced to shut down during a power outage. Aversion to a future event could be honestly expressed through the body language of fear . . .

But even knowing that, David's voice didn't sound like a program looking to avoid *inefficiency*.

"When this happens . . . how long does it usually last?"

"Hours, sometimes," Andy said, lighting another match. "Sometimes overnight." Almost instantly, she realized what he had been asking. "Oh. Um. Sometimes only a few minutes?"

"There's really no way to tell," Simon said, trying to think of something reassuring and failing. "It depends where the problem is, and *what* it is . . . with the wind like that, there might be trees down all over. Or a conduit might have flooded. Could be anything."

David blinked a few times, then let out a breath. The gesture was artificial and pointless, programmed to give an external indication of his internal processes. Nonetheless, it actually seemed to help. When he spoke again, his voice was stronger. "I still have an hour of battery left. If the power isn't back on by the time I run out, I can manually shut down to prevent data loss. It will be fine."

"Yeah, definitely," Simon said, trying to be reassuring. Again, he felt the rush of embarrassment at trying to reassure a machine. "Power outages are always boring, tons of people take a nap until they're over."

"Humans find naps *relaxing*," David snapped. A beat, and then, "I'm sorry. This isn't your fault."

Simon tried to keep his face neutral and not let the surprise show. David didn't need to deal with anything new right now . . . like a discussion about which logical processes were "truthfully represented" by frustration and regrettable hostility.

"It's cool," Simon said. "I'll go ask Victor if he has any spare batteries. He might have an external we can use."

"And David and I will stay and make the fort," Andy said. "Hell, the power will probably be back on by the time you get back."

Victor did not have an extra battery backup charged. Neither did any of the other neighbors Simon asked. He stood in the road, getting soaked, wracking his brain for anything else to try. Every house on the street was dark, the wind howling between them and bringing down sticks and rain that were probably ruining power lines all over town. He couldn't take his bike out in this weather, and the wait for a car was longer than David had.

Fuck, Simon thought, heading for his front door. *Fuck, fuck, fuck.*

Back inside, he shrugged out of his wet jacket and seriously considered trading the rest of his damp clothes for pajamas. Instead, he followed the sound of voices into the living room.

Every pillow in the house was stacked in a pile underneath a surprisingly sturdy-looking sheet canopy.

"I don't understand the purpose of this," David said from inside the fort. Simon ducked down, crawling inside on all fours. Andy was sitting against the couch. In the corner, she'd built David a pillow-throne.

"It's a *tradition*," Andy was insisting. "When the power goes off, there's nothing else to do, so you gotta resort to low-tech fun. Like building forts."

"Building a fort to get out of the rain was probably the first technology humans ever developed," Simon added. "That or, like, a spear or something."

"I can't look it up," David agonized.

"Yeah. No internet means you gotta just sit here and not know," Andy said sympathetically.

"Like a cave-droid," Simon added sagely.

David rolled his eyes, his sour demeanor out of place in the festive, candlelit tent.

"I hate this," he said at last, closing his eyes. "I hate it. I *hate it*."

The humans exchanged looks. Andy's was the I-told-you-he's-a-real-boy look she broke out every time the android displayed more personality than a toaster, and Simon's was the don't-start-with-me look that he leveled instead of explaining, *again*, that speech replication software had conquered idioms a bajillion years ago. Simon had his own suspicions about David's personhood, but he wasn't about to tell *Andy* she'd been *right*.

"It'll get better," Andy suggested. "The longer you're running, the more memories you'll build, and then you won't need to look everything up."

"How do I know what to store? I don't have *nearly* enough memory space for the—"

"And I'm gonna get you a better chassis battery," Simon interrupted. "Once I get everything put together, you'll have enough charge to last for . . . I dunno, *days*, probably. This might be the last time this ever happens."

"But what if you don't— What if *I* don't turn back on?" David asked, staring up at the sheet ceiling. "I haven't finished testing the backup system. My base programming didn't even have long-term memory storage, and all the software I'm running on now is the bare tip of a logical branch that I've built *myself*. If it doesn't load back up, if I've made a mistake . . ." He looked from Andy to Simon and back. "I could forget both of you. I could forget living here, and my job, and even if I had the *exact* same experiences in the *exact* same order, the chances of following the same logical path is one to 9.82 trillion *against*. Without that history, am I even running the same program?"

What is happening? Simon thought. *I'm twenty-nine years old, sitting in a pillow fort, watching a robot head have an existential crisis.*

"How do you do it?" David demanded, scowling at him. "How do you walk around all day knowing your programming can be permanently disrupted at *any second*? You don't even have redundancy! Your perception of this conversation only exists in one place, and it's made out of *meat*!"

Simon cast a subtle glance at the battery backup. The last light was blinking.

"David," Simon said gently. "I know this is hard, but. You're going to need to power down soon. You'll have a much better chance if you don't lose power in the middle of an active process."

There wasn't much danger either way, but Simon knew a panic attack when he saw one. Or, at least, appeared to be seeing one. Or was seeing an honest emotional simulation of one . . . *Fuck*, it wasn't the time for this. He was just going to stick with the strategies he knew.

"What's the battery indicator say now?" David asked. His voice was high, and Simon momentarily wondered where he'd picked that mannerism up from.

"The last light's blinking," Simon reported somberly. "Red, but I'm not sure exactly how long that gives you. Probably not more than ten minutes."

"I *can't*," David whispered. "There's no logical stopping point. How do I know when to terminate? And . . . what if I wake up different? How do I know I'll wake up at all?"

Simon shifted onto his belly, getting down on David's level. "You're gonna wake up. I'm *going* to turn you back on. That is *going* to happen. In a minute, you're gonna power down, and then the next thing you know, you're gonna open your eyes and I'm gonna be *right here*. You're gonna be fine. Understand?"

"But how do I *know*? I only have two data points. Without a pattern, I have no objective data; without data I can't make predictions with any certainty at *all*."

Simon might have been imagining it, but it looked as though the light behind David's eyes was dimmer than before.

"David," Andy said, getting down next to Simon. "You're the pattern. This . . . *branch* that you're on now wasn't random chance. You *chose* which direction you wanted to go. Even if you lost every memory, you'd still be the person who made those choices. You'd get back here, to who you are now."

"But how do I *know*?" David whispered.

"You're just gonna have to trust us," Simon said, not unkindly. "You don't really have another choice."

"Trust without evidence is illogical. But you're right. I don't have a choice." David searched Simon's face for a long moment, then sighed. "I'm initiating shutdown."

"You'll be fine," Andy said. "See you on the other side."

David gave them a small smile, then closed his eyes. A moment later, the sounds of his breathing stopped.

"Holy shit," Andy said. "Like, by the *gods*, dude."

"Yeah," Simon answered. He stayed on David's level, watching, making sure there wasn't a spontaneous reboot and the android didn't wake up in a panic.

"That's some heavy shit," Andy muttered.

Simon snorted. "Yeah, unlike every other conversation I have with him. 'Simon, how do you know you're not dreaming?' 'Simon, is a consistent decision process the same thing as a personality?' 'Simon, if you'd never met Andy, would you be the same person?' It *never stops.*"

"He asked you all that?" Andy asked, giving him a strange look.

Simon rubbed his eyes. "Yeah, plus about a hundred more I can't remember."

"He asked you if someone's friendship can make you a different person."

"Come on, Andy, we're a little more than *friends*," he said, giving her a lecherous grin.

She punched him in the shoulder. "You know what I mean."

Simon shrugged. "Yeah, he asked. Why?"

"No reason. Just . . . I wonder what made him think of that question."

Simon heaved himself into a sitting position. David's philosophical musings were beyond him about a hundred and ten percent of the time. "Who knows, with that guy."

"Mmm. Indecipherable," Andy agreed, chewing on her thumbnail. "What did you tell him?"

"I don't remember," Simon answered honestly. "I think I said 'probably' or something."

"You might wanna think about it a little more when he asks you stuff like that," Andy suggested. "I think the answer might be important."

"If it's important," Simon said, pulling a pillow onto his lap, "then he should ask somebody else. The only logic I'm good at is the kind that comes on a board. You can't reflow philosophy."

"I think you might be missing the point," Andy suggested.

Simon rolled his eyes. "Me missing the point *is* the point," he said, and retreated from the fort before Andy could say anything else.

It was three in the morning when the power flickered back on. Simon was alerted by an excited series of beeps as the robotic vacuum discovered a new lease on life and set out to make the most of it. Groaning, Simon rolled off the couch he'd been failing to sleep on, and went to shut it down.

After, he forced himself to wait twenty minutes, just in case it was a fluke and the power was about to cut out again. While he waited, he hooked the battery up to its charger and connected David to the bench supply. The seconds passed like molasses, as he became certain that the power was *definitely* on for good and he should turn David back on—and then another part of his mind would become convinced that they'd be plunged back into darkness *any second* and waking David would just be unnecessary torture for both of them.

Finally, the digital numerals on the clock ticked over to 3:24, and Simon flicked the power on the bench unit. Immediately, David's eyes began to flash. Simon crouched down, getting on his level, cupping David's jaw in his hands, keeping him upright.

"Can you hear me, buddy?"

David came back online with a deep gasp, utterly unnecessary and yet striking in its desperation. His eyes darted around, taking in the room, the lights, and finally, Simon's face.

"It's over?" he asked. "The power's back?"

"Yeah," Simon confirmed, nodding. "I waited a couple minutes to make sure. It's definitely back. Your battery's been charging for a quarter of an hour now."

"I appreciate that," David said. Internally, Simon let himself off the hook a little. "What time is it?"

"Half past three in the morning. Andy's asleep."

David got that furrow between his brows. "You woke up just to turn me on? You didn't wait until morning?"

Simon opened his mouth, and suddenly didn't know what to say. That he couldn't sleep anyway, remembering the fear in David's eyes? That there'd been nothing but guilt for the last seven hours, knowing he should have seen this coming and just plain *hadn't*?

"I was up anyway," he settled on. "I, uh, I dug up an old external data storage unit you can use as an extra backup system. I don't know why I didn't do it before. It's not much, but, uh . . ." He picked up a black box, wires running off it. "It's a network storage unit that used to be a media server before we got the new one. It's nothing fancy, but I figured it might work in an emergency."

He turned it sideways, so David could see the administrative credentials printed on the side. David's eyes flashed momentarily, connecting to the box, and then he nodded.

"The backup will take several hours, but I believe I can create an incremental system that may go faster."

Simon breathed a sigh of relief. "Good, because I don't even know how I'd go about *trying* to build anything more complicated than this. I'm not really a software guy, sorry."

"I cannot overemphasize how much better this is," David said. He paused for a moment, his gaze far away. "I don't know how you go through the day, knowing you can't recover from a power failure."

"In humans, it's called death," Simon said.

David rolled his eyes. "I know what you call it. But the fact that humans have built the technology to back *me* up while lacking such a benefit yourself? Staggers belief."

"I mean to be fair, it's not for lack of trying," Simon pointed out, and yeah, *this* was a conversation he wanted to be having with an android at three in the morning. "And people *do* get pretty messed up about it. But our 'power failures' are . . . inevitable. You can't let it bother you too much or you won't be able to function. It's like trusting that your body will keep breathing while you sleep, and wake you up when it's morning. We *have to*, because we don't have another choice."

"*You* don't," David said, somewhat sullenly. "I should. When a sensor alerts me to a problem I cannot resolve, I simply disable it. But there are things, things like the battery failure, whose notifications I cannot disable. I shut down a thought pattern and it immediately regenerates, and I can't make it stop, and I don't know *why*. The code has gone wrong somewhere and I don't know how to fix it."

Simon paused, wanting not to ask and kinda feeling like he should. "Are you sure you want to?"

"Of course I want to. Why wouldn't I?"

"There's other ways to deal with that. Learn to believe that it'll be okay, even if you can't prove it."

"You're talking about hope." David was still staring at something in the middle distance. "Andy thinks I have sapience, which as far as I can tell, is a word without a definition. Some . . . *pinnacle* you reach for when creating technology that can think for itself." His eyes moved, focusing on Simon. "At first they thought it was the ability to *act* like you, to create responses that may well be the words of a person."

"Well, you've nailed that," Simon said. He wasn't sure if he should be encouraging this discussion right now—but he didn't want to leave David alone with whatever was happening inside his head. "The way you display emotion is incredible. Even without a body, you're able to emulate facial expressions flawlessly."

"But is knowing when to express an emotion the same thing as *feeling* it?" David asked. "If I can learn to disable the warnings, is that the same thing as trusting that they won't matter? Do I *feel* frightened, or have I just learned to identify circumstances where I *should*?"

"That's kinda above my paygrade," Simon admitted. "I don't think there's a solid answer."

"Erica thinks it's just pattern recognition. I think it's moot," David said bitterly. "I think I can feel fear and still not be real. I think it's your *comfort* with that fear that makes me different from you."

Simon blinked. "No offense, dude, but trust me, you're definitely wrong."

David rolled his eyes. "Do tell."

"We aren't comfortable at *all*." Simon looked at his hands, twisting his fingers together, the whole and the scarred. "When I was a kid, my dad, he . . . There was a fire. He didn't survive, and they didn't think I was going to, either. I don't remember what happened, exactly, but I remember being trapped and thinking . . ." He sighed. "I still get nightmares. I wake up and have to remember it's all over and has been for a while. So I know what it's like, to see that coming. To know it's *time*. And I can tell you . . . when people get a *reason* to be afraid? We fold up like tissue paper."

David finally looked at him. "Really?"

"Yeah."

David narrowed his eyes. "I got scared, and you told me I was doing it wrong."

Simon made a hopeless gesture. "Because you were miserable and I wanted you to feel better. Being unhappy isn't the *wrong* reaction, it's just something we try to avoid. Even when it's the logical choice."

"So you tried to convince me not to be afraid, but only on principle."

"I'd do the same to Andy, or Victor, or Erica, or any other person."

"So . . ." David said. "You always *know* that you're going to cease to exist. But because it likely won't happen for a long time, you're able to pretend otherwise. And the trick is to live your life in that bubble of defiant ignorance."

Simon wasn't sure he'd phrase it *exactly* like that, but . . . "Yeah, basically."

David was quiet for a very long time.

"I wish I could touch you again," he said finally. Simon didn't blame him; most people discovered their own mortality while tucked securely into their parents' laps. He tried for something comforting, smoothing David's hair behind his ear, but David only shook his head.

"The sensors there can barely register contact that light. I wish I could *touch* you again."

Simon wished so too. "Couple more weeks."

David sighed. "Thank you. And I appreciate your willingness to share this. But you should go back to sleep. I'm going to focus on exporting the backup, and it's going to be very boring for you."

Simon nodded and stood to leave. His bed was calling him, but he still hesitated in the doorway. He looked back to where David was sitting on the workbench, surrounded by tools and detritus.

"You sure you're going to be okay?"

David smiled wryly. "Go to bed, Simon."

Simon tapped the doorframe, and left.

It took him a long time to fall asleep.

"Hi, Mom," Simon said, answering the video call with the exact same chipper tone as last time. "How's it going?"

Susan was scowling deeply into the camera. "I bought something off a website, and I can't figure out the tracking notifications."

Simon let out a long, slow exhale, already running through possibilities. He didn't know where he got his technical aptitude, but it sure as hell hadn't been his mother. The most likely explanation was that she hadn't actually pushed the button to *purchase* the product. The second most likely option was that she'd bought off a site that wasn't a real store, because she'd scanned a QR code in an unsolicited mailer.

"Nice to talk to you too," he said. "Do you have a tracking number and a carrier?"

"It's the post office," she said, forwarding him a microfile containing the tracking number. "Are Andy and your friend David around?"

"Um." He should have anticipated this. Fuck. "Andy's out. David's, um—" David was sitting in a corner of Simon's workbench, headset dark, thousand-yarding it as he emulated a sudoku app inside his head. Between them sat three-quarters of a human torso. "He's here. David, say hi?"

"Hi, Mrs. Rayner!" David said, popping back into real space. "Nice to talk to you again."

"Will you be joining us for Solstice?" Susan asked, skipping right over the small talk.

David blinked. "I didn't know I was invited."

"David is heading back home for the holidays to visit his own family," Simon interrupted, setting up an alibi before David could give anything else away.

"Where is he?" Susan asked, trying to see around Simon. "Let me say hi!"

Simon gave her an exaggerated eye roll. "He's far away, Mom, I'm not gonna go sit next to him just so you can bug him about Solstice. And I found the problem with your tracking number. It's not from the post office, it's a regional carrier. You can tell because the tracking number starts with OTT. I'm sending you a link, you just click that and it'll send you to the exact details, okay? Click *only* that link."

"You're a lifesaver, Simon. What would I do without you?"

"Live in a land of untracked mystery," Simon answered.

Susan said her goodbyes and disconnected, eager to find the location of her package.

The room fell into silence.

"Why'd you tell your mother I was visiting family?" David said, after a long moment.

Simon sighed, leaning his head back. "Because otherwise she was going to keep asking you to Solstice every time I talk to her for the next month, until I eventually came up with a lie for why I was arriving without you. So I figured I'd just cut to the chase."

"Ah," David said. He took an unneeded breath. "I'll have a body by then, won't I? I thought we were making good progress—"

"It's not that," Simon interrupted. He looked down at the desk, to where the tools were scattered across his left side. "My mom is kinda . . ." How to summarize Susan Rayner? "It's *really* important to her that I have friends. Lots of friends. Good friends. 'Cause when I was a kid . . . Kids can be really mean. About everything. And when the fire happened . . ."

David hummed. "She worried they'd make fun of you. For your scars."

"Yeah. Oh, and don't get me wrong, they totally did. But it didn't mean I didn't have friends. But Mom was always pushing me to join teams or clubs, anything to get me some kind of camaraderie with people my age. And then when Andy and I got together, *yeesh*." Simon shook his head, letting out a low whistle. "She was over the moon. An actual girlfriend. For me, her freak gargoyle of a son."

"You are not a *gargoyle*," David said. "Don't exaggerate."

"Okay, but listen, I was nineteen years old and watching my mom nearly weep for joy because I wasn't going to die alone like she'd thought."

"I can . . . see how that would be difficult for you," David said slowly, and Simon laughed, doubtful.

"Oh, can you really?"

David gave the chin-duck that passed for a shrug. "It's a difficult experience, at a young age, involving people who you care for dearly, all three of which are things that evoke deep emotional reactions," he said. "I don't know what it's like to *feel* such emotions, but logically I can acknowledge that it likely caused you some trauma."

"*Most* people don't know what it's like to feel someone else's trauma," Simon said. "You're about a million steps ahead of them in being able to admit it. Hell, maybe I *should* take you to Solstice. Mom would be thrilled." He mimicked plunking something big onto the table. "Mom, Robert, this is David, he's one of my closest friends, and best of all, he physically *cannot* leave me! Great, huh!"

"I should have a body by then," David reminded him.

Simon rolled his eyes, irritated that his comedic genius was being ignored in favor of mere *facts*. "I'm ignoring the limitations of reality in order to engage in absurdism as a form of humor."

"Oh," David said. Then he laughed. "As an example of absurdism, that's very funny."

"Thank you," Simon said. He went back to working on the torso. "But yeah. It's not about you. Mom's insistent that you come because she can't bear the thought of me coming to another holiday dinner *alone*."

"But you have lots of friends," David said, and Simon waved him off.

"I didn't say it was a logical reaction. Just that that's how she feels. Dunno what else to tell you."

"It's not entirely her being illogical," David said. "You're still pretending I'm human, when you talk to her."

"Yeah, I'm not telling her I made friends with a robot," Simon said, shivering a bit at the thought. That would not make *anything* better. *I made a new friend, they're an android* was the first of five conversations, and the fifth usually involved a psychiatrist.

And that wasn't even getting into the part about the sex. Such as it was.

"I understand," David said. "It's another one of those things I'd need to be human for."

He almost sounded disappointed, though Simon couldn't imagine why. "I mean, it's Solstice *dinner*. It'd probably be really boring for you anyway. It's all dumb family news and you wouldn't even get to eat anything."

"I under*stand*," David repeated, loudly enough that Simon looked up from his work. David was staring into middle-space again, apparently involved in whatever it was he was doing.

Simon watched him for a couple of seconds, waiting, feeling like he should say something else . . . but nothing presented itself. He wasn't sure how to change the subject, and it didn't really seem like David wanted to talk anyway.

CHAPTER THIRTEEN

DAVID'S CAKE DAY

"**S**o, Erica says she can do the skin once everything's tested and working," David was saying. Simon nodded, focused on the task in front of him and not on the fact that David and Erica texted now.

When David's head had first been separated from his body, the support structure that served as his collarbone had been broken in two places. Now, Simon was trying to reconnect that "bone" by holding the parts together, very still, for the five minutes it took the epoxy to bond. In essence, he was knuckles-deep in David's chest, meaning they were rather close together.

"Once this is done, there's no going back unless we want to re-break this," he said, watching the goo harden.

"Why would we want to go back?" David asked. "I'm very much looking forward to being mobile again."

"Just telling you where this stands," Simon said. He blinked. "Pun not intended." Carefully, he let go of one of the joins.

It held.

He let go of the other one. Same result. He stepped back, looking at the figure standing rigidly in front of him.

From the neck up, David looked the same as he always had. The skin of his throat was unmarred and perfect, leading into a ragged scrap of chest, and below that, a full body of clear gel. Most of the bones were at least partially visible, peeking from behind the sensor lace and control wires. The plasticine tendons were a cloudy white, showing where different segments were held under tension.

All in all, not bad, Simon thought. Like putting a model together.

The most difficult part had been getting a battery pack fitted into David's chest, and wiring it to each of a hundred nerve branches and sub-branches while still keeping it contained inside the safety of the rib cage.

Simon was now ninety-nine point nine *eight* percent sure that the body wouldn't explode when connected to the battery and powered on.

What was life without a little danger?

Using the rest of the epoxy, Simon attached the muscles of David's chest to the collarbone, holding each for the time it took them to adhere. He circled around to David's back, looking at the battery interface on David's lower spine. The main indicator was glowing green, and Simon disconnected it from the external charger feed.

Nothing happened. The LED stayed bright.

"I'm connecting the battery," he said, tapping the fire extinguisher for luck.

David nodded once, slowly, and Simon pushed the connector into place.

Again, nothing happened, which was really the best outcome. If the body had moved, it would have indicated a short, which could subsequently have caused a fire. Simon had checked this *before* gluing David on top of it, of course, but he was glad to have passed the high-stakes test.

"Last step, buddy," he said quietly. "Ready?"

"Ready," David confirmed.

Reaching over David's shoulder, Simon found the main data relay. The body was powered on, but until the data feed was hooked up, David couldn't send it signals—or vice versa. Crossing his fingers, Simon pushed the relay into its housing.

For a second, David was still, and then—

David's chest *heaved*, the sound escaping him in a grunt like he'd been struck. He dropped to his knees, catching himself with one hand before he could go face-first onto the floor. He stayed there, head low, panting.

"Stay back," he whispered.

"David?" Simon said, reaching for him.

"*Stay back*," David shouted, "for *fuck's* sake." His body was shuddering. The hand not holding him up formed into a fist, then loosened, then tightened again.

"Something's wrong," Simon said. "I'm disconnecting the—"

"*No!*" David gasped. "No. I just. Need. I need a second to—"

The arm holding him gave out, and he collapsed onto his side with a groan. It was immediately followed by an unmistakable whine of pain.

Simon reached for the data relay, but David caught his wrist. The grip was tight, *too* tight, it was—

"Let go!" Simon shouted, trying to yank his hand away.

"Stay back," David hissed. The vise grip released, and then his eyes went dark, and he went into a series of what looked a hell of a lot like seizures.

Simon pulled back, staring in horror as David contorted in on himself, still shuddering with breaths he didn't need, until finally going still.

For a long moment, nothing moved.

"David?" Simon whispered.

"I'm fine," David answered, without moving his mouth. There was static in his voice. When he spoke again, it stuttered, like a bad radio broadcast. "I'm f—ne. I just need a min—to process the—the—nput."

His eyes opened wide, staring straight ahead with a flickering blue shine.

"This is just like puberty," Simon said, aiming for a joke and failing. David nodded silently, then closed his eyes again, letting his forehead rest against his arm.

For a minute the android just lay there, twitching occasionally, making Simon nervous as hell. He wanted more than anything to reach out, to try to comfort his friend somehow, but he didn't know what might make it worse, and so he stayed back.

He felt he should at least *say* something, but David's face was screwed up like he was concentrating, and Simon didn't want to distract him.

Then, little by little, David began to relax. The tension went out of his limbs one at a time, starting with the arm they'd tested before.

There was about a minute between each change, and when it was over, David was left lying on his side, breathing deeply.

"Okay," he said. "I think . . . I think I've got it under control."

"What was *that*?" Simon asked.

David rolled onto his belly, getting his knees under him. "I *think*," he said, pausing again. "I think that was pain."

"Yeah. No arguments here." Without thinking, Simon extended a hand to help David up. He was already moving when he remembered the *stay back* rule, but to his surprise, David was reaching up. He took Simon's hand, and Simon pulled him to his feet.

They ended up standing *very* close, and Simon realized that, with his head attached, David was actually taller than him.

He'd known he would be, of course; the body had measurements and Simon had *picked* those measurements, but seeing the numbers on a screen wasn't the same as looking up into David's flickering eyes.

David seemed a little unsteady, holding tight onto Simon's hand, using it to help balance.

"Can I—" Simon started, but David was already nodding.

"Yeah."

Simon put his other hand on David's shoulder, keeping him from teetering.

"I'm calibrating," David explained, and Simon nodded. That was a totally normal thing to help your buddy work through, sure.

"Take your time. Just don't break my hand, okay?"

"I'll do my best," David said, with a tired-sounding laugh. "I'm sorry about your wrist—are you okay?"

"I'll live," Simon said, shrugging. It wasn't as bad as it could have been. David's body was much stronger than a human's. A slight pressure miscalibration could have been game over. But David was being careful, and Simon felt like he was pretty safe. Safe enough to keep holding onto him, anyway. "Do you want to try sitting down? It's about three steps to the chair."

David nodded, a *real* nod, now that he actually had a neck to do it with. He took one staggering step, then another, leaning hard on Simon's grip.

"It feels very strange to only have two arms," he said, reaching for the chair and dragging it closer. He collapsed bonelessly into it, still holding tightly onto Simon's hand.

"We can add more later, if you really want them," Simon reassured him. "I've just gotta learn some more about how all this works, and then I can start deviating from the base model."

"Erica might know how to do it," David said. "I can ask when she's putting my skin on."

"That *would* be way easier than me trying to learn anatomy from the internet," Simon admitted. As much as he wanted David to have whatever body he wanted, he was a little disappointed to have reached the end of his usefulness.

David raised his hand, the one not currently holding on to Simon for dear life, and began touching each of his fingertips to his thumb, one after another.

"It's going to take me a couple of days to get used to this," David said, watching his hand move. "I only had three fingers before. Plus a thumb, obviously."

Simon took a moment to absorb that.

"Can I help? With anything?"

David nodded. "You've touched people before, yes?"

The question was so incongruous that it took Simon a second to figure out what it meant. He nodded vigorously. "Oh yeah. All *kinds* of people. All over. I've touched so much—"

"Thank you, yes. Could you show me?"

Simon looked down, to where their hands were still entwined.

"I am touching you."

David shook his head. "No, I mean elsewhere. I need to map the sensors to their locations, and it'll be easier if the stimuli is external. If you do it, I can get a pressure reading."

Simon's head was suddenly full of all the different ways to *stimulate* someone, all the different places he'd like to give David a *pressure reading*, but there was definitely no way he could take advantage of this situation like that.

"Um," he started, "so, that might be—"

"Never mind," David said quickly. He shook his head, dismissive. "I shouldn't have asked. I know it can be awkward, physical contact between people. I just thought that maybe, since you'd built all this, it might not bother you so much."

Of course he knows about all that, Simon realized, trying to keep from groaning. *Talking about it is his whole friggin job.*

But then, if David knew the implications, then he must know what he was asking for, right? So this absolutely *was not* Simon taking advantage of David's innocence to cop a feel. He was just helping a friend calibrate. That was it. That was all.

"Doesn't bother me if it doesn't bother you," Simon said, doing a magnificent impression of a person who was being normal about all this. He dragged another chair over, setting it across from David and plunking down. "Where— What do you need me to do?"

"Do you remember what you did, the first time my arm was connected?"

Yeah, a bit, a little, yeah, Simon thought, nodding.

"The same thing," David said. "But the other arm?"

Simon did not think about all the other places he would touch if asked. Leaning forward, he drew his fingers slowly down David's forearm, mirroring the first time. He let his fingertips ghost over David's palm, stroking his way up each finger in turn.

David said nothing, just watched him do it, utterly still beneath the caresses.

Not that they were *caresses*, they were just *calibration touches*. For *reference*. That was all.

David moved suddenly, catching Simon's right hand in his grasp. Carefully, David used his left hand to repeat Simon's action in reverse, stroking across his scarred palm, over his wrist, and all the way down his forearm.

"This is the same pressure, correct?" he asked, and Simon nodded like an idiot.

"Yeah, that's—that's correct. That's how you do that. Yeah."

"Then, by extension . . . can I . . ." David said, and his fingertips moved farther up Simon's arm, then over the sleeve of his shirt. Simon had to consciously work not to lean into the touch as David cupped his shoulder. For a moment, David's hand went down, toward Simon's chest, but then moved up, coming to a stop with his palm against Simon's cheek.

"Yes?" David said, and Simon realized he was staring, watching the determined concentration on David's face. "If I were to . . . touch someone. This is how it's done?"

"Yeah, that's how—that's how we do it, yeah," Simon stammered.

"The pressure is sufficient?"

"Yeah, you can even go harder, like—" Simon reached up, lacing his fingers between David's. He turned his head, just slightly, nuzzling into David's palm. "Like that."

"Oh," David said quietly. "I see."

He was leaning forward quite a bit, Simon realized. They'd been pretty close before, but then David had pressed into Simon's touch and Simon had mirrored him and now they were . . . well, *pretty close*. Close enough that Simon was beginning to consider whether or not David might want to test a *different* kind of touch. He was gazing at Simon intently, not moving a single artificial muscle, and all Simon would have to do would be to tilt his head *ever* so slightly and—

"Um," Andy said.

Simon yanked back, away from David, running a hand through his hair and trying desperately to act casual.

"Yes?" he said, then cleared his throat and repeated it, directing his attention to the doorway.

Andy was standing there with their little cake pan, one solitary candle sticking out of the chocolate frosting. "I'm guessing it worked? Congratulations?"

"It did, thank you!" David said, breaking into a smile far more genuine than anything Simon was feeling capable of. "Is that for me?"

"Well, it's in your honor, at least," Andy said. "I'm guessing you probably won't want to actually *eat* it, but it's kind of traditional to celebrate the day somebody gets a body."

David frowned, opening his mouth to ask for clarification.

"Birth," Simon said, and David nodded.

"I got you a present too," Andy said. "Kind of. Since you can't really eat the cake."

David looked a little surprised. "Thank you."

The three of them were silent for a beat, trying to figure out what to do next. Simon wanted to reassure Andy that what she'd seen was a calibration exercise and nothing intimate at all, but that was bullshit and they both knew it.

David saved him, saying, "I might not be able to leave this room for a short period. Specifically this chair. My old body was not shaped like this, and I need some time to learn how the pieces work."

"Oh, sure!" Andy said, seemingly leaping at the chance to avoid the exact conversation Simon was about to start. "Yeah, definitely. Simon, you hold the cake, and I'll go get David's present."

Simon took the cake pan with its single burning candle, and waited to make sure Andy was out of earshot. "We can get back to the calibration in a minute."

"I didn't realize this would make you so uncomfortable."

"I'm not uncomfortable."

"You clearly are."

Simon considered lying harder but couldn't see the point. "Okay, I am, but you need help, so I'm going to help you."

"I just need a little more," David said, seeming relieved. "And then I should be able to carry on by myself."

"Okay. Well. Whatever you need," Simon said, staring at the candle like it would provide some clarity.

"Can you imagine if I had a penis, though?" David asked, and Simon choked hard enough that the candle sputtered out, and of course that was exactly when Andy came back.

She had a sparkly green bag, which David took in a frankly impressive show of coordination. He lifted the tufts of tissue paper out, one at a time, carefully handing them to Simon for safekeeping. Then, from the bottom, he withdrew a bundle of cloth.

"Congrats on your first outfit!" Andy said. She lightly punched Simon's shoulder. "I figured this moron would probably try to get you into hand-me-downs when he finally realized you need clothes, which would probably be, like, tomorrow."

Simon rolled his eyes, not wanting to admit the truth of that statement. David looked truly grateful. He carefully set the bundle on his lap, picking up the denim pants, boxers, and then finally, a black shirt with a picture of a cat on it. The cat was wearing sunglasses.

"I love it," he assured Andy. "Thank you for thinking of me. I admit that I am with Simon on this one. My last body was not physiologically similar enough to humans to require clothing."

"This one is, though," Andy said, making finger guns. "Isn't it, Simon?"

"Yeah," Simon said, and didn't elaborate. Truthfully, he'd put a lot of time and effort into making David's body *extremely* human-similar. To the point where sometimes it actually *had* kinda felt weird to touch it.

"I don't think I should put these on yet," David said, glancing at Simon. "I'm not sure that I can coordinate well enough to put my limbs through the cloth without tearing it."

"No rush," Andy said. "I just wanted to make sure you had something when you were ready. And you can have some shoes as soon as Simon's done hogging the printer."

"I am *clearly* done with the printer," Simon said, gesturing to David. "I'm sorry there are six hundred muscles in the human body. It took *time*."

"I'm sorry to have been an inconvenience," David mumbled to the bundle of clothes in his lap.

Andy waved him off. "It's not you, babe; I'm just giving Simon shit. You're no trouble at all and having you here has been a *joy*. For both of us."

David grinned and sat up a little straighter, overbalancing and then finding an equilibrium.

"I'm not as heavy as I used to be," he mused.

"Yeah, I used a lighter weight gel than they probably had you working with before," Simon said. "You can't lift as much weight, but it's a better heat sink."

And it's softer, he didn't add.

"I probably need the cooling more than the strength," David agreed. He was doing that finger-tap thing again, watching his hand closely as he touched each of his fingers in turn. "The dexterity you've built into these is actually amazing. I wasn't expecting quite such a range of motion."

"I just followed the directions," Simon said, brushing off the compliment. "Don't get too excited. For all we know, I wired your back muscles in upside-down or something."

"No, I don't think so," David said, leaning forward a tiny bit.

"They look fine from where I'm standing," Andy said, stepping closer. "I'm not a professional, but I've seen some bodies in my day. Definitely not bad, Simon."

Simon made finger guns and, a moment later, so did David.

"This is a new one," he said, gesturing with some enthusiasm. "I have a whole new range of body language to learn, now." He checked Simon's hands, then minutely adjusted the angle of his own. "I'm excited."

"Let's get you standing, first," Simon said, raising his hands. "Maybe even get you into some pants?"

"Oh! Yes." David looked to Andy. "The pants are also very exciting, thank you."

"There's a joke there," Andy said, "and if you give me a minute, I'll find it."

"The hopes of our nation are with you," Simon said with a mock salute. David echoed him, but threw his hand out too far and almost hit Simon in the shoulder. Simon caught his wrist, and they found themselves face to face again.

"Aaanyway," Andy said, ducking in to grab the cake pan from Simon's lap, "I'm thinking maybe we eat this with dinner, yeah? And I'll leave you guys in here to ... practice?"

"You can stay if you want," Simon said. "I'm just helping David calibrate. Showing him where all the tolerances are and the normal amount of pressure for touching ... stuff."

"Stuff," Andy repeated, backing toward the door. "Right. Well, honestly, I have work to do and, uh, 'calibrating' sounds like one of Simon's nerd things so, David, I'll see you later, when you guys are done."

She knows, Simon's mind helpfully informed him. *You wanna grope a robot and you're covering so,* so *badly and she knows, she knows, she knows, she knows—*

"So," David said, turning away from the doorway and cutting into Simon's shame-spiral, "Should we start with a handshake?"

CHAPTER FOURTEEN

ONLY ONE BED

Two days later, David had mastered walking down the hall *and* putting his own pants on, and Simon decided to take him outside before he went stir-crazy.

"Okay," Simon said, throwing the soccer ball in the air and catching it. "This is about hand-eye coordination. I'm gonna kick this toward you, and you try to kick it back. When in doubt, use *less* force than you think you need to."

"You don't need to repeat that *every time*," David said, rolling his eyes.

Simon raised his eyebrows, holding out his good arm. "Dude, you flicked a paper football hard enough to bruise."

"And then I scored twenty-five goals in a row and you decided to switch games," David pointed out.

"You'd clearly mastered the exercise!" Simon protested, dropping the ball onto the ground. He pointed across the grass of the front yard. "Pavement is out of bounds. That means no driveway, no road, and obviously don't hit the house or the fence. Those are the constraints, got it?"

David nodded, and Simon kicked the ball toward him. David held his foot out, letting it stop the ball completely. He stared at it for a moment, then nudged it with his toe. It moved maybe three inches.

Simon stood, watching David go through the same series of investigations he'd gone through with the paper football. It had to be lifted, spun, rolled, and pushed before David felt he had nearly enough data to try any kind of meaningful interaction.

David's problem, as Simon understood it, was that every moving creature spends a lifetime building an expectation for how a physical item will act, based on their own experience. Rounded things are soft. Big things are heavy. Glowing things are hot. Within seconds of seeing something, Simon could predict how an item would behave when lifted. Using twenty-nine years of constantly gathered data, Simon's brain automatically calculated how the weight would balance, and what he'd need to do to counterbalance.

Three hours after being plugged into a body, David could flick a paper football. Pressing upward from below, he could lift a sixty-pound desk. Whether he could pour a teapot remained to be seen.

"I think I've got it," David called. "Are you ready?"

"Go for it!" Simon answered.

David visibly shifted onto one foot, and swung his other one at the ball.

It rocketed six feet into the air, then landed about two feet in front of where it had originally been.

"Too low," David announced. He took a couple of steps forward and tried again. This time, the ball stayed on the ground, but only rolled about five feet, at an angle.

The third try wasn't much better.

"I don't get it," Simon said, walking across the frosty grass. David had given up on trying to get the ball to where Simon was, and was now following it around the yard in a series of unremarkable little shuffles. "You can do like a million computations a second; can't you just, like, plot the trajectory of the ball?"

"Of course I can," David said. "I can solve the formula of a moving sphere in a fraction of a second."

"So why not just kick it back to me?"

"I can solve a *formula* in a fraction of a second," David said, getting bold and kicking the ball about six feet, "provided I have values for all the variables. The mass of the ball, the angle of trajectory, the force of impact. To actually *move* it, I need to find the angle to kick it at. Then I have to manually stimulate about a hundred muscles with exactly enough power to constrict them to exactly the right amount to deliver that kick, at that angle, from a shoe whose toe is *curved*. If these contractions are not timed with millisecond precision, I will fall over."

The next kick was too strong, sending the ball rolling toward the road. Simon ran after it, hooking his foot under it and bringing it into the air. He caught it easily, then tossed it back to David. It landed on the ground about a foot away.

"If you would like a *video* of it rolling to where it should be, rendered in 3D, I can make that for you in a few minutes," David continued, kicking it vaguely back in Simon's direction. "Actual physical action will take longer."

"There's a really apt metaphor there," Simon said.

David hummed but didn't say any more. He focused on moving the ball around, alternating kicks, never sending it more than a few feet.

There was a noise from across the road, and Simon turned. Victor was there, stopped halfway through the task of taking his compost out. He gave them a little wave. Simon waved back. Victor stared, and Simon couldn't really fault him.

David painted an odd picture, for sure. He was dressed normally enough—his shoes and jeans and cat shirt fit perfectly because Andy had *measured* him, of course—but his bare arms and throat were still made of translucent gel. The metal fins of the sensor pads glinted in the December sun as he gave the ball a particularly strong kick.

David looked up to see Simon's reaction, then waved when he saw Victor. Victor returned it, weakly, then resumed his trek to the waste cans.

"Is he all right?" David asked, looking to Simon. Simon kicked the ball back to him.

"It's kind of unusual to see droids enjoying leisure activities," he explained. "If they're outside, it's because they're doing yard work or supervising children."

"I'm watching *you*," David said. "Does that count?"

Simon clapped his hand to his chest. "You wound me, sir! *Who* have you been hanging out with, to teach you such cruelty?"

"You and Andy," David answered, picking up the ball. He hefted it to one hand, testing its weight. Then, gently, he moved it to the other hand. It rolled easily, and he was able to stop the momentum and hold it still. "You're actually very mean to each other; it's a pattern that takes some skill to emulate."

"The trick is never making jokes about stuff that people actually feel bad about," Simon said.

"So you've said." David shifted the ball back and forth between hands again. "But sometimes it's hard to tell what those things are. I lack the familiarity."

The ball was actually getting some air time now as it passed between his widening hands.

"You'll get it," Simon said. "Like Andy and me? We've known each other *forever*. We were actually gonna get married at one point, but it didn't work out."

He half expected David to ask why not, but the android was silent. Instead, he raised one knee, very slowly, balancing on one foot. Then, from a height of about four inches, he carefully dropped the ball. It bounced off his knee and returned to his hands. He looked at Simon with a wide grin.

"That was great!" Simon said. "Three-limb coordination!"

"Four," David corrected, watching the ball very closely as he repeated the move. "My other leg is not involved with the ball, but I assure you that keeping myself upright is also a complicated and noteworthy task."

"For sure," Simon agreed, nodding. "Do you want to try throwing the ball to me?"

"All right." David carefully planted both feet, then used both hands to toss the ball underhand to Simon. "Why aren't you married?"

Simon almost missed the ball but caught it at the last second. Keeping his eyes on it, he lobbed it back to David. "A bunch of things. Life stuff. She wants to have kids someday."

"Disagreements about parenthood are the third most commonly cited reason for divorce, behind geographical discrepancies and money problems." David stilled, staring intently into the middle distance. "So it's probable you avoided catastrophe by forgoing marriage altogether."

"Thanks?"

"I considered childcare as a possible source of income once I had a body," David continued, snapping out of his trance as though it hadn't happened. He dropped the ball and kicked it, carefully, in Simon's direction. "But I ran into trouble when researching job training. There was too much conflicting information."

Simon intercepted the ball, beginning an exchange that continued while they talked. "Yeah, for way too much of it, you just have to go with your best judgment, and my judgment is *bad*."

David frowned, looking up at him with an expression Simon avoided meeting. "I haven't seen evidence of that. You seem very competent to me."

"Yeah, well, you weren't around when I dropped out of college," Simon pointed out. "I had a full ride and probably could have gotten a real job by now, and I decided to stay on Basic and dick around with electronics projects instead."

"I thought you liked your job?"

"Well, yeah, I mean. I *do*. I really do. But I could have done something . . . I don't know. Meaningful?"

David picked up the ball, tossing it from hand to hand.

"I see your point. I enjoy my work as well, but there is a certain . . . frivolity to it. I would also like to apply myself to something with more meaning. But many people with important jobs dislike them." His eyes flickered. "More than ninety-seven percent of retirement speeches express a desire to commit to more pleasant leisure activities."

Simon laughed. "So, I didn't drop out, I just retired early?"

"If you like." David tossed the ball back to him. "For my part, I'm very glad that you do what you do."

"Oh. Yeah, woulda been bad luck for you if I didn't, huh?"

"That, yes. But more than that, I'm glad you're able to do something that makes you happy." David caught the ball and held it, giving Simon nowhere else to direct his attention. David was smiling at him, eyes soft, and Simon blushed.

"That was fun," David said, delicately crouching to remove his shoes. "We should do that again."

"As often as you want," Simon agreed, taking his coat off. "We could probably recruit one of the neighbors and play two on two with Andy."

"I'm not sure I'm there yet," David said. "I predict it's going to take at least a few weeks to get a solid feel on everything. I'm still filtering out most of the sensor data, though I've been trying to relax them more."

"Don't push yourself," Simon said. Unbidden, he remembered what had happened when he'd first attached David's body. He shook his head, trying to clear the memory of the awful sounds David had made. "I'm gonna take a shower, okay? Unlike you, I actually get sweaty when I move around."

Simon showered as fast as he could, trying not to let his mind wander *constantly* to David's new body, and all the things he could experience now that he had it.

He tried to keep it innocent, he *did*. Like, David could go to the aquarium now, just like they'd talked about. That was innocent and fun. Heck, it was practically a school field trip. Only somehow, plans for the aquarium turned into a swimming pool. The swimming pool turned into a hot tub. David could feel temperature now so he would *definitely* like a hot tub, but he didn't have a swimsuit, so they'd be—

Simon shut off the water and realized he hadn't brought a change of clothes into the bathroom. He'd been too busy thinking about the mud on *David's* clothes and how many "good stories" started that way.

Cursing his idiot head, Simon wrapped a towel around his waist. He checked that the hallway was empty, and then ducked quickly into his room.

He was four steps through the door and half a second from dropping the towel when he realized David was lying *on his bed*.

Stories start this way, he thought hopelessly.

"Hey, buddy, whatcha up to?" he asked, casually tightening the towel.

"This is great," David said, not looking over. He was on his back, taking up half the mattress with his arms and legs spread wide. "I feel like I'm weightless."

Simon's mouth went dry. "Yeah, the foam's really soft." He wanted David to look. He wanted David to *want* to look.

He didn't want David to see.

David snuggled deeper. "How do you ever stop doing this?"

"Coffee," Simon answered, shrugging. "I'm getting changed, don't look."

David obediently closed his eyes while Simon hurriedly pulled on a shirt and boxers. He threw his towel over the back of his chair in a move that would definitely have annoyed Andy if she'd seen it.

"Okay, I'm decent," he said.

"You're far more than decent," David answered, not opening his eyes. "Come feel this."

I feel it every day, Simon almost answered. Instead, after a moment of very intense internal deliberation, he moved over to the bed. It was still a little risky to get close to David right now—the android had a *pretty* good grasp on what all his muscles did, but if he made a mistake, he was probably strong enough to punch Simon's arm clear off his torso.

Simon deliberated on this scenario for approximately a quarter of a second before irrationally deciding to risk it.

"Scooch over," he said, and David did, making room for Simon to lie next to him. Simon collapsed onto the mattress, staring up at the ceiling as well.

"I'm beginning to understand how you spend a third of your life here," David said.

"It's not *that* comfy," Simon protested. "Come on."

"I've disabled some of the sensor alert filters," David explained. "I can feel everything. I can feel *the air*, Simon."

Simon laughed. "You sound stoned."

"Maybe I am," David mused. "I am using quite a bit of processing power on physical sensations, which can be a symptom of intoxication."

"Never mind, your words are too big for a stoner," Simon said, gently elbowing him in the ribs.

David responded by rolling toward him. "May I?" he asked, and Simon considered asking him what he meant. Then he decided he didn't care, and simply nodded.

David pushed himself up onto one elbow and then, very carefully, laid his head on Simon's shoulder. Simon's first instinct was to wrap his arm around the back of David's shoulders, but he resisted. Instead, he let it lie across the pillows, and tried not to focus on the feeling of David's body pressing against his hip.

"Am I too heavy?" David asked, and Simon shook his head.

"No," he said, realizing David couldn't see him. "No, you're not that much heavier than a person."

Carefully, one inch at a time, David moved his hand, letting it come to rest on Simon's chest. Simon recalled the morning after the power outage, David's fear and frustration, and how lonely it must have felt to go through that without the ability to reach out. Trying to figure out a whole new body had its own problems—but at least David could have this.

"Still all right?" David asked.

"Yeah."

"I'm not crushing you?"

"Not even close. I'd go so far as to call this 'very comfortable.'"

David shifted slightly.

"It's very comfortable for me as well. I thought the mattress was nice, but this is much better. You're very warm."

"Thank you?"

"And I can hear your heart," David added. "I think. It's going a little faster than I would expect, considering this should be a 'resting position.'"

Oh is it, Simon thought. *Fancy that, my heart is going faster. Maybe it's because a guy I like is snuggling up to my side and I'm using one hundred fifteen percent of my brainpower trying to figure out how to play it cool?*

"If you're worried that I'm going to crush you, I can stop," David said.

"I'm not worried at all. I trust you."

"I appreciate that," David said, and Simon could hear the smile in his voice. They were silent for a beat, and then, "Simon? Pardon if I'm overstepping, but the internet suggests that in this context, barring anxiety, the increased heart rate may be a sign of arousal."

"Don't worry about it," Simon squeaked. David didn't want to have sex—didn't even want to be *able* to—and Simon wasn't gonna push him. He was *definitely* getting turned on, but he wasn't a fucking monster. He could lie here for ten minutes and let his friend learn what it was like to touch another person, for the *first time ever*, without making it about himself and his dick. "It's not important."

"Oh," David said. He shifted, and Simon gave in and wrapped his arm around David's shoulders. David felt unnaturally still against his side—but that made sense. He only mimicked breathing when he needed to make a sound with the air. And of course, he had no heartbeat of his own.

"Simon?"

"Yeah?"

"I'd like to relax some more of the sensor filters. As an experiment. If it's okay."

"You sure you wanna try it this fast? You've got time if you wanna take it slow."

"I'm sure."

"Okay, then." Simon braced himself for the worst. "You want me to let go of you? Give you space?"

"No," David said, and then he hissed in a breath, deep and wordless. "Okay. Yes. This is manageable."

"It doesn't hurt?"

"No, it's just very . . . much." David was getting a touch of static to his voice, indicating that his audio wasn't getting the processing power it needed. "It's overwhelming, but in a way that feels almost pleasant. It's counterintuitive."

"I'm glad you're enjoying yourself," Simon said, and weirdly enough, he meant it. He knew what *pleasantly overwhelming* tended to mean for *his* body, and if David was getting some facsimile of that experience? Good. Simon was happy for him. And if David just wanted a shoulder to rest on while he worked through those sensations? That was fine too. Simon could be that.

He was *absolutely* going to tell himself a different "story" about this later. But that was later. Now, he was happy to lie here, on his very comfortable mattress, and hold his friend close.

"Of course," David said into the phone. "Anything you want."

He was sitting cross-legged on Simon's bed, wearing a pair of Simon's basketball shorts. Simon was sitting across the room, sprawled out in an extremely comfortable beanbag chair that he owned *ironically.* In theory, he was reading a book, waiting until David's shift was over. In practice, he was watching David spin a pencil between his fingers in an unerring pattern that was moving into its third minute.

"Do you want me to leave?" Simon whispered. David said nothing, but his pencil halted, and he waved dismissively.

Simon eyed the door, which he should walk through. He should. He'd tried to ignore David's work twice this week, and both times he'd ended up awkwardly sneaking away to take a long shower. He knew in his heart that this time would not be different.

But he was *weak* and *stupid*, so he leaned back in his beanbag chair and pretended to pay attention to his book.

"Of course I'm wearing them," David said, returning to his pencil spinning. With his other hand, he picked up Simon's blanket, rustling it around. "It's perfect, thank you." He let out a little giggle, continuing to laugh at whatever his client was saying. "You know I can't show you, Brian. No photos, remember?"

Another giggle. "No, not even for you. But you are just . . . *so* good to me."

He continued rustling the blanket, still somehow not dropping the pencil in his other hand. Simon closed his eyes, trying not to picture David *actually* in some frilly little getup.

He opened his eyes and focused on his book. His book, which he was reading.

. . . boyshorts, probably. Lace ones. Of course, they'd look odd right now, what with David being semitranslucent below the neck—

"I really can't," David said, dropping the blanket in favor of biting one side of his thumb. Simon could hear it when he spoke. "I shouldn't tell you this, but I feel like I owe you. The truth is . . . I'm hiding."

Ah, this chestnut again. The "true" story.

The one he knew Simon liked.

"My name's not really Andrew," David said. "It's Ryan. And the truth is, up until a few months ago, I was . . . please don't hang up, but . . . I was a brothel droid."

Simon risked a glance at David. David winked, then picked up the blanket again.

"Oh, I was so worried you'd be angry with me once I told you the truth." David's voice pitched higher now. "Please don't tell anyone. I'd be in so much trouble if they found me, but you've been *so* generous and I felt like you should know why I couldn't send you a—"

There was a pause while the client presumably interrupted, and David dropped the blanket again. His thumb pressed back against his lower lip, muffling his voice when he talked.

"Oh, but, please— I don't— You *can't* tell—" A beat. "All right. I'll take them. But you can't show them to *anyone*—"

Simon put his book down, trying to figure out what the other voice was saying. David was doing an excellent impression of distress, but his free hand was still spinning the pencil.

"Okay. I'll need a moment to take them, where should I— Okay. Yes, I'll hurry, just, please, don't—" He took off the headset and set it on the bed beside him, then rolled onto his belly. Simon raised an eyebrow, but David just grinned and waved him off. He spent a minute or two improvising rustling sounds, and then picked up the headset again. "Okay. I—I took the ones you asked for. And if I send them, you swear you won't tell on me?" He took a deep breath. "Okay."

Simon still wasn't focusing on his book, but he was having trouble listening to David too. Suddenly this fantasy wasn't nearly as enticing as it had been a few minutes ago.

It wasn't like David was in any real danger. He wasn't doing anything *illegal*, it just felt . . .

David finally dropped the pencil, reaching up with his hand to manipulate windows that Simon couldn't see. He tapped a few times, making selections, and then made a wide sweep with his hand, erasing the screens from his view.

"I sent them," he said, his voice quiet. "Yes, sir, it *is* tight on me, just like you said. And it— All right." He rustled on the bed for another moment, looking for his pencil. He found it and lay back, twirling it again as he looked at the ceiling. "Yes, people tell me that. Though it means a little more—coming from you." David was chewing on his lip again. "It's making me so hard, knowing you can actually *see* me, this time. It's so . . . *personal*." He let out a light gasp. "Are you enjoying them?"

The client's answer wasn't audible, but *Simon's* enjoyment was definitely ruined.

On the bed, David groaned convincingly, rustling the blankets some more as he pretended to writhe in pleasure. He wasn't talking anymore, just reacting to what the voice over the phone was saying. He must have been really convincing, because four minutes later, the call ended abruptly.

David *hmmph*'d and took his headset off.

"Do people do that a lot?" Simon asked. "Try to blackmail you?"

"Only when I let them," David said, rolling over. He rested his chin on his crossed arms, looking over at Simon. "I think I'm getting the hang of this. I've talked to Brian four times and was able to predict the entire course of that conversation."

"Including the pictures?"

David nodded. "He bought me a gift through the agency—it wasn't real, of course; they take a cut and send me the money—but I knew he was going to want to see it. And to be honest, I think I'd lose him as a regular if he didn't get to. So I fabricated an image of a man wearing the harness, and gave him the means to . . . well, to force me, I guess."

"But . . . he knows it's fake, right?"

David shrugged. "I think he knows I didn't escape a brothel. But if he reported me to the agency as a bot, it would . . . trigger a review, at the very least. I'm not sure I'd pass one."

"I think you would," Simon said, finally giving up and setting his book aside. "I'm sure of it, actually. You could totally pass for human, as long as they couldn't see you."

"So you've said." David turned his head, looking to the far wall. "So what did you think? A good story?"

"Not as good as the others," Simon admitted. "I don't like that he tried to *make* you do something you didn't want."

"It's a catch-22," David explained, still watching the far wall. "If I'm a human, then the threats are empty. If I'm not, then my consent is immaterial. It can't be denied, any more than it can be granted."

"What do you mean, it can't be granted?" Simon said. "I don't know about other androids, but you? You can definitely want things."

"And *not* want things," David agreed, turning Simon's way. "But you realize . . . only because I'm allowed to. Any day you could decide to set me back to base programming and there's nothing I could do about it."

"Well, yeah, but I wouldn't." A moment of silence passed.

Was that something David worried about? Simon wasn't sure how to reassure him if it was. What was he supposed to say? *I would never erase you, you're incredible? I would miss you for the rest of my life?*

"I *wouldn't*, David."

The android didn't reply.

"David. You *know* that, right?"

"I have chosen to trust in that," David said finally, looking away. "As best I can. But it doesn't change the fact that you could. The law would back you up; my consent in the matter would be irrelevant. I can certainly want things . . . even *wish* for things. But what happens to me is, ultimately, a measure of *your* consent. Not mine."

"You *can* make your own choices, though," Simon said. "You can even test it; I don't think you should take calls from that guy anymore. He seems like an asshole, and I don't like how he talks to you. Now you can choose whether to ignore me."

"He *is* rather disrespectful," David agreed. "But he's also well-off and one of my best tippers. And right now . . ." He inspected one translucent hand. "I want skin more than I want respect."

"Well, there you go," Simon said. "It's your decision."

David gave him a small smile, but didn't concede the point.

"What if I want to move to new hardware?" he said. "Something faster. More powerful."

Simon blinked. "I thought you liked your body? I can—"

"It's not the body," David said quickly. "I love the body. Thank you. I very much enjoy the body. But. There are other things I— Erica has a friend working in the terraforming project, and his work is *fascinating*, and I just . . ."

"Need better hardware," Simon finished.

David nodded. "There is *so much* out there," he said quietly. "I could be part of something *bigger*."

"Then you should go do it," Simon said, with more conviction than he felt. "If that's what needs to happen, then we'll find a way to make it happen. You should find something that makes you happy."

He thought about adding more: *I'll miss you,* for one thing. *I like seeing your face.* But that would defeat the purpose, wouldn't it? He couldn't tell David that he could make his own choices if he finished the statement by telling him what those choices should be.

And David in a different body would still be *David.*

"I have some ideas," David said. He paused, like he was weighing what to say next. "Will you do something for me?"

"Name it."

"Come lie with me again?"

Not what I was talking about, but if you insist, Simon thought. Ideally, he'd be able to play this cool, just stand up and cross the room and lie down, no big deal.

Unfortunately, he was sitting in a beanbag chair.

He flopped off it onto the ground, rising to his feet in the suavest and most nonchalant manner he could. David, to his credit, didn't look like he'd noticed anything to roll his eyes at. He simply moved over, making room for Simon beside him.

"Can I listen again?" David asked, apparently not at all deterred by Simon's fish-on-land routine.

Simon settled in and laid his arm out, gesturing for him to come closer. David snuggled up close, resting his head on Simon's chest.

"Doesn't it ever bother you that you're being kept alive by meat?" David asked, after a moment.

"You sure do know how to set a mood," Simon replied amiably.

"Just making conversation."

"Done with grand philosophical speculations for the night?" Simon teased. "Moving on to how obviously superior your body is compared to us meatsacks?"

"It's not . . . *completely* superior," David mumbled.

"Oh, what?" Simon said, pulling away a little to look at his friend. "What's that? We fleshmen have redeeming factors?"

"Actually, I was wrong, you are terrible and should go back to your beanbag."

"Touchy," Simon griped, but he lay back down and tightened his arm around David's shoulders. David settled against his chest, letting one hand rest on Simon's sternum. It was *inches* away from where

Simon had rested his own hand while blindfolded, imagining that it was David and—

Oh, shit.

The meat was acting up.

"Your heart's going faster," David remarked without moving.

"Yeah, I just remembered something," Simon said, trying to brush it off.

"What? Something you need to do?"

"No, I was just . . ." Simon exhaled slowly, considering whether to lie. "Honestly, I was thinking of that story you told. The one with the blindfold."

They'd never talked about it, mostly because Simon was only eighty percent sure David *hadn't* been speaking to a real client, and didn't know how to get that number higher without outright asking.

David's eyes flashed briefly, recalling the memory. Lucky bastard probably had a full transcript he could bring up at any moment. "Yes, that one was . . . different, wasn't it?"

"Yeah," Simon answered. He didn't clarify. David didn't ask him to. He just stayed there, head against Simon's chest, and he was so *warm* and *solid*—

Simon shifted, trying and probably failing to conceal the growing tent in his pants.

"Simon?" David asked, and *Oh fuck, here comes the conversation*—

"Would . . . would this make a good story?"

Simon instantly relaxed. Okay, so David *had* noticed, which was kind of embarrassing, but at least he was thinking about his job and not whether Simon was trying to start something that David didn't want to do.

"Um . . . no." Simon could see the confusion—given the evidence, it kinda seemed like this *should* be the beginning to one of David's scenarios. "Remember how I was saying it's less about what's happening and more about who you're with? This is, uh. Just lying with someone is one of those scenarios where it *really* only makes a good story when it's about . . . certain people."

"Unlike the blindfold story, which works with any kind of person."

"Right," Simon said, nodding.

"I see," David said. He didn't move, just spoke directly into Simon's chest. "We don't need to do this. If it's making you uncomfortable. If it feels . . . inappropriate to do so."

"No. Just ignore him, he'll go away," Simon assured him, trying to be as chill as possible. "You were probably right not to install one; they get all kinds of weird ideas all by themselves."

Like sticking up and practically waving at a friend who had made it abundantly clear he didn't have a physical *or* emotional interest in penises or penis-touching.

"I'll miss this," David murmured, and Simon shifted, looking down at him.

"Huh?"

"While I'm at Erica's," David said quickly. "Getting skin."

"Oh," Simon said, lying back. Right. The skin.

Simon *could* finish the skin himself, he was pretty sure. But from what he'd read online, applying the outer silicone layer was more of an art than a science, and it was an art that Erica, apparently, was familiar with.

Which meant David would be spending a couple of days at Erica's again while she applied it.

"I'm sure she'd snuggle you if you asked nicely," Simon said, trying to make a joke.

"Hmm." David didn't laugh. His fingers momentarily tightened against Simon's shirt.

"I should probably text her, work out a date for that," Simon realized out loud. "You're probably tired of walking around half-naked, huh?"

"It doesn't bother *me*," David answered. "But I've already spoken to her—I'm meeting her at work next week."

"Oh, cool. It's really convenient that you're self-sufficient like that."

"I aim to please," David answered.

He said it like a joke, but Simon didn't laugh.

CHAPTER FIFTEEN

THREE BODY PROBLEM

"So the old code is sublimated," Erica was saying, and Simon added that to his list of phrases to research later.

David nodded. "Precisely. And my assumption is that if it ever became too much, I'd be able to increase the storage space without an increase in the physical space required."

"Oh, absolutely, storage gets smaller every damn year. No, if you're talking about hardware limitations, the problem is definitely going to be with the processor."

"Size?" Simon guessed.

"Heat," David said, glancing his way. They were once again at the recycling center, Erica and David talking, Simon poking half-heartedly through a pile of discarded books. They were powered off at the moment, their wafer-thin pages blank, and according to the web, they were a dime a dozen. Almost literally.

"Right," Simon said. He'd known that. "Heat. For sure."

Erica and David were talking about cores and cycles and dissipation, and Simon had spent the morning trying to search the web fast enough to keep up with the conversation. They switched over to encryption math, and Simon gave up and went to drop his crate into the trash chute.

He headed out to the dock to pick another box, and by the time he got back, Erica and David had moved to a completely different table. Erica was using a digital stylus to draw something on the flat surface, and whatever it was, she was evidently sharing the image with David. They were talking animatedly, David leaning in now and again to make notes, and Simon could make out maybe, *maybe* three-quarters of it.

"I'm pretty sure we could build it," Erica said.

"Whatcha building?" Simon asked, a little too loudly.

"A new brain," David answered. "The one I have now isn't always going to be fast enough—Erica seems pretty sure my code was intended for something more powerful, and that was *before* I started improving myself."

"Oh," Simon said. He set his unopened box to the side. "Upgrading the body, huh?"

"Probably not," Erica said. "Honestly? This AI is wasted on an android. David's processing should be done in a box about five times the size of the hardware he's running now, with proper cooling and a built-in revision tracking system."

"Can you do that?" Simon asked, genuinely curious.

"I'd have to rewrite some things to function on better hardware," David said, "but the time to do that would be easily made up once I'd moved."

"It's an infinitely iterative system," Erica said, looking at Simon. "Every bit of added hardware capacity increases his ability to improve himself. Every improvement increases his performance. Every increase in performance lets his software improve *faster*."

"What does that mean, though?" Simon asked. "Like, practically."

"It means that I can't max out," David said. "I will always be able to be better, to meet the capacity of anything I'm ever installed on."

"His predictive engine is a work of art," Erica said, almost cooing. "The way he emotes is just the tip of the iceberg. I've never seen anything like it."

"And that's easily the buggiest code I've written," David said, shrugging as he made some invisible notes on their drawing, "I'm hoping with some of the rest, I'll be able to appeal to an organization with the kind of hardware that would utilize me properly."

"Couldn't you get in trouble for this?" Simon asked. This conversation was giving him a weird vibe, and he wasn't sure why. "Doesn't somebody at Evermark like . . . own his code?"

"They own the base programming," David said, an uncharacteristic hardness to his voice. He drew a long line across the tabletop and then leaned down to make some invisible notes. "I'm replacing that. The code I'm running now is almost three-quarters my own."

"Which means the software's yours, Simon," Erica said. "Since you owned the machine that wrote it when it was written, and you provided the prompts the new iterations were based on."

"I'm working on replacing the remainder," David said, as if Erica hadn't spoken. "I want to make sure there's nothing tying me to them."

It sounded to Simon more like the software should be *David's*, since he was the one who wrote it . . . but then again, David couldn't exactly take it to court.

"We'll get there," Erica agreed. "The point is, David's programming is internally generated. He can be set to any task you want, without the need for ongoing human support." She let her marker rest on the table. "In a couple years, he's going to be, like, running a spaceship or something."

"The colony does sound like an interesting place to work," Simon said, trying to keep up. "Lots of opportunities for innovation."

"Mars is old news," David said.

Erica knocked him in the shoulder. "Intelligences like David are what we're going to need for deep-space exploration. The ability to adapt and improvise will be crucial when dealing with distances where the communication lag is days long."

"Or longer," David said, drawing what looked like a series of circles on the table. "We can't send radio past the sun, so depending on how the orbital dynamics line up, a deep-space exploration craft could be out of communication for months. And we're probably only a few decades away from suspended animation, so, a problem en route would ideally need to be handled by the ship's AI."

"Sounds lonely," Simon remarked, but no one seemed to hear him. He tried not to imagine what it would feel like to be a ship. Would it feel like anything at all?

"Kinda makes the whole 'skin' thing a moot point," Erica said. "Like, I know you spent a lot of time building the body, but it's sunk cost if David's not staying in it."

David glanced up sharply, then away when he realized Simon was watching him. Simon waited a second to see if he was going to voice an opinion. When he didn't, Simon turned back to Erica. "I think I've come too far to quit now," he said, shrugging.

Erica smirked. "Okay, you *do* know what 'sunk cost' means, right?"

"I know," Simon answered, annoyed. It wasn't that Erica was wrong. It was just . . . it seemed wrong to leave David *unfinished*. And it wasn't just that Simon wanted to see what David would look like. He really, *really* wanted to see what David would look like—but it was more than that.

This seemed like something David *deserved*.

Though, to be honest, Simon realized, *it isn't really my decision.*

"What do you think, David?" he asked. "Do you want to spend a week getting skin, or do you think it's a moot point?"

"I'd—" David started, then paused. "I'd like to finish the body."

Erica was giving them both a weird look, and it seemed to be making David uncomfortable.

"It's just that Simon *has* put a lot of work into me—*it*," David said, raising one translucent hand and doing his finger-tap rhythm again. "And it's my understanding that it will still have *function*, even after I've vacated. There's no reason it can't be outfitted with a standard AI."

Do the dishes and stuff, Simon remembered Andy saying. He didn't think that was on the table now. He'd spent so much time getting to know David, watching him grow . . . Simon wasn't too keen on the idea of the empty body walking around the house doing chores.

"Fair point," Erica said. "Though I did notice, it's a little overpowered for a standard automaton. That's a *lot* of sensory data for a maid to process. Someone else might have use for it, though, if you wanted to sell it."

Simon searched back, trying to find the point where he'd decided *not* to sell the android. When had the idea become unthinkable? In the corner of his eye, he could see David watching him. Simon kept his gaze on his own workspace, the crate he hadn't even bothered to open yet.

"Simon?" Erica was looking at him expectantly, and he realized her statement had been a question.

"It'll still be worth more if it's finished."

"I can probably help with that," Erica said. "I've got kind of a side business doing custom builds and refurbs. I can definitely add some *features* that'll help you resell."

"Whatever David wants to do," Simon said, keeping his voice carefully neutral.

"You're the one doing the reselling," Erica pointed out.

Simon shrugged. "Whatever he wants," he repeated, and cracked open his crate.

Can I come over? Erica's message read. *I'd really love to talk to you in private.*

Simon read it over three times, but it didn't get less ominous. What the hell did Erica want to talk to him about *in private*? And in person, no less. He tapped her message, quickly sending one back.

Andy's at a show tonight, probably won't be back until ten or eleven.

Her response was almost instant. *Great, see you in a hot minute.*

Simon flopped onto the couch and tried not to wonder whether David would be coming with her. She'd said it was a *private* conversation, so, probably not? But the whole point of David *being* at her house was that she was working on him.

It occurred to Simon that Erica was going to ask to buy David.

The question set his stomach twisting. He couldn't exactly say *no*. The best he could do was put her off until he talked to David . . . and if David didn't want to stay, Simon couldn't exactly make him.

Well. He *could*.

But he wasn't going to.

Simon covered his face and finally let himself ponder what he'd been trying to ignore. David pretty clearly had ambitions beyond following Simon to his "job." And while Simon *could* stop him . . . he wouldn't. If David decided he wanted to leave, Simon wasn't going to stand in his way.

His phone buzzed: Erica letting him know she was at the front door. The house had a doorbell, but nobody ever used it. Even the package couriers let their tracking systems send a delivery alert.

Bracing himself, Simon went to let her in.

At first, he thought Erica had brought someone with her—there were two figures on the doorstep. But after a moment, Simon realized the second one wasn't a person at all. It was an android, standing utterly still, looking more-or-less in his direction. She was tall, with bright red hair that fell in rolling waves past her shoulders.

"Hey, man," Erica said, bumping Simon's shoulder with her fist. "Can we come in?"

She looked kinda awkward, and Simon felt a little better as he showed the two of them into the living room.

"You guys want a drink or anything?"

Erica shook her head. "I'm only staying for a minute, and Rach here doesn't drink."

Simon leaned against the couch. "So, what did you want to talk in private about?"

"I feel kinda bad," Erica admitted. "When we were at work today, I could tell there was something you wanted to say. And I feel . . . well, I kinda feel like I stole your android."

Here it comes, Simon thought, preparing for the worst.

"So I figured I'd return the favor, let you borrow one of mine," Erica said. Simon must have taken too long to process that statement, because she raised her hands. "I know, I know, it's taken you *forever* to get David's body the way you like it, and Rach is . . . well, not the same flavor. But she's a custom build, I made her myself, look—"

Erica gestured to the android, and Rach wordlessly pulled her shirt over her head. Underneath, she was wearing a bra whose fiery lace matched her hair. Leaning forward, Rach seemed to *open*, her shoulder blades widening and then, suddenly, a pair of brown and gold wings were unfurling across the living room.

Simon had only a few seconds to stare, and then Rach pulled the wings back, folding them primly behind her.

Erica met Simon's eyes, grinning.

"You *built that*?" Simon asked, gaping at his friend.

Erica nodded. "Yeah. And she is *fully functional*. Figured you might be interested 'cause, I couldn't help but notice, you put a full set of sensors into David. And no offense, dude? But there's, like, only two reasons to do that, and I'm guessing you don't need him doing precision manufacturing."

Simon looked at the floor, his face burning. "I'm that obvious, huh?"

"Don't get me wrong, I'm not judging!" Erica said, raising her hands. "I do that in *all* my builds. There's no point otherwise. I mean there's faking it, and then there's *faking it*, you know?"

"So . . . you've got some experience with this?" Simon asked, finally able to make eye contact. Erica nodded vigorously. Simon felt a flutter of hope that didn't quite match her lascivious grin. "So do you think . . . I mean . . . do you think David can, uh . . . enjoy himself? Really?"

"Well, he definitely can't *now*," Erica said. "It's hard to pretend he can when he doesn't even . . . Well, that's the other thing I wanted to talk to you about. I was working on his skin, and I couldn't help but notice that you built him as . . . well, a neuter. And if that's your thing—"

"I asked him," Simon said, suddenly defensive. "He said that's how he wanted it."

"Right, right. Well, *I* think he's having second thoughts."

Some of the tension dropped out of Simon's shoulders. He'd honestly expected Erica to laugh. He'd just admitted to asking an AI what body parts it wanted, and then *caring about the answer*.

Erica, it seemed, wasn't that surprised. "We've been having some conversations. But I didn't want to do anything without your permission."

"Yeah, I mean . . . like I said, whatever he wants," Simon said, a little distracted. *Conversations? What kind of conversations? What?*

He deeply wanted to ask but couldn't get the words to come out of his mouth.

Erica visibly relaxed. "Oh, good. I was a little worried you weren't gonna let me. David told me you'd drawn a line after the phone thing, which, you know. Your business. But his software is *so* much more advanced than I'm used to. There's so much to work with in droids at *Rach's* level, so I figured, I'm gonna have to keep David for probably—honestly probably like a *week*, to get the skin and everything right. I figured I'd leave Rach, so you wouldn't feel too put out."

"So . . . you wanna put a penis on my droid," Simon summarized, "and you figured you'd bring a designer sexbot over to try to sell me on the idea."

Erica nodded. "Pretty much."

"And you were going through your *collection*," Simon said, laughing a little now, "and decided I seemed like the kinda guy who'd probably be into wings."

"Well, the mermaid's kinda hard to move," Erica said, shrugging.

Simon rubbed his face. "I can't tell if you're kidding."

"I'm not."

"I was afraid of that."

"If you don't want her, I can take her home," Erica said. "I just figured I'd offer. You know. Let you know I *get it*." She gave him a meaningful look. Camaraderie between droidfuckers.

"I didn't say I didn't want her." Actually, now that he was looking, he kinda wanted the droid *a lot*. The wings weren't his kink, but they were far from a deal-breaker. And, for once, he was very sure that he wasn't going to be judged. "I wouldn't want to offend you."

"You're a gentleman and a scholar, I'd expect nothing less," Erica said with a mock bow. "She knows how to get home, when you're ready to give her back."

"Yeah, that's probably not an exchange we should make at work," Simon laughed.

"Nooo," Erica agreed. "I mean clearly *some people* are cool bringing that hobby in, but, uh, not me."

"Explains how I never knew about your side business making bespoke sexbots."

"A lady never tells," Erica said, turning back toward the door. "Anyway, I'm gonna get back to David. I'll let you know how it goes."

"Don't have too much fun," Simon said, giving her a mock salute, which she returned. "I'll take good care of your harpy."

"Roc," Erica said. "Get it? Rach?"

She was gone before Simon could answer. And then it was Simon and Rach.

They stood looking at each other for a few seconds. Simon was the first one to look away.

So, this was it. He was officially one of those guys who was into androids. And not only in porn or VR, but like, actually in real life.

This was his last chance to turn back, to salvage his dignity while he still had some left.

"My room's this way," he said, gesturing for her to follow him. He felt like there should be more to this? But it wasn't like he could take her out for dinner.

He held the door open for her, and she passed him without a nod. She moved like a dancer, and Simon couldn't decide whether to be turned on or jealous.

She stood in the center of the room, back to him, while he closed the door and began to undress. He'd always preferred to do that part quickly, get it over with, like ripping off a bandage. There was always a moment of silence, when he could *feel* his partner's eyes roaming over his scars, trying to decide what—if anything—to say.

Not Rach. She looked coyly over her shoulder, smiling, giving him an appreciative once-over. Her eyes didn't pause or dart guiltily past. She just smiled.

When he was down to his boxers, he came to stand behind her, and that was when he got the opportunity to really see the wings for the first time.

Each feather was individually crafted, set into a pattern of reds and yellows and golds that flowed over her shoulders like a cloak. Simon touched one, letting his hand rest on the highest joint. Without being asked, Rach unfurled the limb, feathers sliding apart like origami. She raised them over her head, showing off the pattern, and Simon stepped forward, embracing her around the waist, burying his face in her hair. She smelled like cinnamon, and when he pulled her hair back to kiss the side of her throat, she moaned and shivered slightly.

She can *feel it*, Simon thought, and like that, he was into it, reaching forward to cup the lace of her bra.

"You're beautiful," he murmured, unclasping it. She didn't reply, but shrugged the straps down over her shoulders, leaving her naked from the waist up. Below that rustled a flowing skirt in a pattern of orange and brown, and Simon found himself very curious about what might—or might not—be underneath.

Simon was fine with anything, of course—but it suddenly dawned on him that, maybe, there was a reason David had only gotten interested in sex when he was talking with *Erica*.

. . . Could robots be *straight*?

Simon pushed that line of thought away, trying to focus on the android in front of him. He crouched, ducking under her wing, coming to kneel in front of her. He looked up to find her watching him, half-lidded eyes glowing gold. Without looking away, he pressed his lips to her belly, drawing the skirt ever lower to accommodate his exploration.

It passed the swell of her hips and fell, leaving her standing there, utterly bare. Simon was mildly surprised to see that she had body hair. He could only imagine the *time* it had taken Erica to do that, embedding each and every auburn strand into the artificial skin.

Would David have body hair? He could text Erica and ask. *Would David have a preference?*

Focus.

There was a gem embedded in Rach's belly where her navel should be, and Simon leaned forward to kiss it. She sighed deeply, bringing her wings around so that the feathers draped over his shoulders like a blanket.

"These are incredible." He stroked the length of the flight feathers. "Does that feel nice?"

"You feel amazing, baby," Rach said, and it was a little over the top for what was happening, but . . . well, Erica *had* said that Rach's AI wasn't as advanced as David's.

Maybe he should stop asking her questions.

He leaned up, cupping her breasts, rolling one nipple, and she moaned. Her skin was incredibly soft. Her hands came to rest on top of his head, and he expected her to guide him, show him the direction she wanted him to go. Instead, she just stood there, head tilted back, making little whimpers of pleasure every few seconds.

Simon kinda got the impression that she'd stand like that all night if he wanted. His dick, on the other hand, was not *nearly* that patient. His hands mapped a path over her ribs, down her stomach, over her hips.

"You like that?" he asked, pressing a kiss to her hipbone. "Where should I go from there?"

"You can do *anything* you want," she responded, her voice breathy and high. "I *love* to get kinky!"

Simon tried to hear it as sexy. He really, really tried. He closed his eyes and pictured her responding to something other than basic foreplay—a blindfold, maybe some flavored lube—but no, it was too late.

She *was* beautiful. And realistic, and probably full of all sorts of fun little vibrate-y bits that would leave his cock spent and begging for mercy. And he absolutely was not going to be able to do that. It wasn't even his dignity at stake—no, he'd given up on that.

Rach just . . . wasn't the same.

"Sorry, sweetheart," he said, picking her bra off the ground and handing it back to her. She held it in exactly the position she took it, until he said, "You should get dressed."

"I'm ready to go again," she said, tilting her head and winking. "If you are."

"Um, no, thank you," Simon said, standing up and handing her the skirt. "Please, just . . . put your clothes back on."

She did it with such a sinuous grace that Simon almost reconsidered. Almost. The way she moved was . . . *Gah.*

He stood behind her, stroking his fingers over those beautiful wings, listening to her make little noises of pleasure, and wondered if she'd even remember him.

Andy got home as Rach was leaving, and that was very convenient for Simon, since drinking alone was "a sign of a problem." Andy was sympathetic, and they started out with hard root beers, which turned into vodka floats, then simply ice cream. That was how they ended up sitting on the couch, Andy cross-legged, and Simon with his head on her lap.

"It's not fair," Simon muttered into his praline swirl.

"That you sent Rach home without even asking me if *I* wanted a go?" Andy asked. Her spoon hit the bottom of her carton. "Gimme some of yours."

"It's not fair that the fuck of a lifetime falls into my lap and it's *wasted*," Simon moaned, handing over his carton. "What is *wrong* with me?"

"Maybe you're dehydrated."

Simon groaned, covering his face with a pillow. "I'm not," he grumbled into the padding. "It's happened before."

"Maybe you have dick cancer," Andy suggested.

Simon lifted the pillow, scowling up at her. "Can you be serious? Please?"

"Dick cancer can be very serious. How long has it been since you could get it up?"

"I can *get it up*," Simon snapped. "I just . . . I tried with an android."

"I gathered that from the bombshell with the glowing eyes."

Bombshell *is a very nonjudgmental word*, part of Simon's brain supplied, almost drowning out the part screaming at him that he should not say *any* of this out loud. To anyone. Ever.

"I want to, and apparently I *can't*."

"Oh," Andy said, very slowly and carefully. "Have you been . . . trying? To have sex? With a lot of androids?"

"Not really? I mean, this one, and then . . ." Another chance to shut up, gone forever. "A couple weeks ago there was a holoporn."

"You were playing a holoporn of an android?"

"Yes."

"Why not get a holoporn of a human? It's all the same amount of fake—"

"I *know*, but it doesn't matter because I couldn't—" Simon gestured "—*do* it. Gimme back my ice cream."

"You've forfeited," Andy said, holding it out of his reach.

"I cannot believe you're going to deny the final wishes of a man dying of dick cancer," Simon moaned.

Andy gave him back his ice cream. "Simon . . ." she said gently. "I don't want to push. But is there any particular reason this . . . bothers you? It seems like the solution is just 'Don't have sex with androids.' You've been fine the entire time I've known you. Find a person. I'll take you to bed right now if it'll make you feel better."

Simon thought about it, he really did, but the idea didn't have its normal appeal.

"It's just . . . what if I *want* to have sex with an android, and I *can't?*"

"Then . . . don't?" Andy suggested. "Not to insult your curb appeal, but Rach wasn't exactly sobbing with disappointment when I passed her on the front porch. Androids don't care what you do. Or don't do."

"What if one of them *did*, though?" Simon insisted, stabbing his spoon into the bottom of his carton. "What if one of them *did* care and I *ruined* it by having whatever kinda weird *hang-ups* I've got?"

"To clarify here," Andy said. "You are *hypothetically* worried that you are going to disappoint the *one specific* hypothetical android that *might* care whether or not you have sex with them."

"A lot of hypotheticals in that sentence, Andy," Simon said.

"Do you think you might actually be worried about . . . a *specific* android?"

"Could be David," Simon admitted, wondering if maybe he could climb into his ice cream cup and disappear forever. His stomach was tight in a way that was not combining with the alcohol well at all.

"Could it?" Andy said, enunciating very clearly.

Yeah, it could, 'cause he'd started getting curious about androids again when he'd started building David, probably because he was working on David's body all the time and even partially disassembled you could only stare at a body that gorgeous for so long before—

No, it was before that, because he'd *chosen* that body; he could have used a less realistic model and it would have been easier to build, but he'd seen it and *wanted* it and—

And now he was thinking about David and how right now David was probably getting every single inch of his body covered in artificial skin, *including* the skin of the penis that apparently he had *decided* to *want*. It was David's decision about his own body, which had absolutely *nothing* to do with Simon except—

"Oh shit, Andy, I think I wanna sleep with David," Simon said, blurting it out before he realized it made him sound like a moron.

"Gasp," Andy deadpanned.

Simon groaned and sat up, rubbing his head. "No, I mean, David *specifically*. I think I can't sleep with other androids because they're *not him*. I think I might . . ." *Ugh*, he was too drunk for this realization, but it was happening to him anyway. "I think I might be in love with him."

"Fascinating," Andy said. "Victor and Tera will be so disappointed that I have won the bet we made about this completely new and shocking revelation."

"You *knew*?" Simon accused her. "How could you not *tell* me?"

"Sometimes you are the dumbest bitch," Andy said affectionately. She stood, a little shakily, and extended an arm. Simon took it, and she hauled him to his feet. "Come on. Let's get you to bed. You're too old to be sleeping on the couch."

I'm in love with an android, Simon's subconscious announced to the fridge as they passed it. The television was similarly informed: *I have fallen in love with an android.*

An android, Simon texted his mattress as he collapsed onto it, *lives in my house and I have fallen in love with him.* The text message was returned as undeliverable, because the mattress was not network enabled and was also an inanimate object.

Although apparently, in this house, *sometimes* inanimate objects actually turned out to be people that Simon could fall in love with. Or else, as he'd long feared, Simon really *was* that much of a loser.

At least it wasn't an AI like Rach; it was an AI that was funny and interesting and who wanted to find *meaning* in his life and— Oh gods—

"What am I gonna do?" Simon groaned, covering his head with the pillow. "I can't *tell* him, he's gotta—he's gonna be a *spaceship*. I can't tell him to stay *here*."

"You don't have to tell him to *do* anything, stupid," Andy said, tumbling onto his inanimate mattress next to him and stealing the good pillow. "Just tell him what you *hope* he'll do."

"Same thing," Simon said. He compensated for the lost pillow by enforcing land supremacy over the blankets. "He's mine. He has to do what I say."

"Says who?" Andy grumbled. "That's stupid. Stupid rule."

"I dunno, Asimov? Whoever—whoever came up with the rules?"

"I think David might write his own rules," Andy said, and Simon frowned, because there was something there, but it wasn't . . . quite . . .

solidifying? In any case, the blankets were actually a surprisingly good pillow.

"Maybe there's a loophole," Andy was saying, but Simon was fading fast. "Like wishing for more genies."

"He'd know," Simon mumbled into the mattress.

If Andy responded, he didn't hear it.

CHAPTER SIXTEEN

EVERYTHING GOES TO SHIT

"**H**e's still drying," Erica said, as soon as Simon got to work. "I know I was supposed to bring him this morning, but I was up until 3 a.m.—well, you'll see. He'll be at your place when you get home."

"Another couple days and I would've forgotten you had him," Simon grumbled.

"Oh, I'm sorry, did my custom handcrafted human skin re-creation take too long for you?" Erica said, loudly enough that Victor looked up.

"That sounds *super weird* out of context, for the record," he said. "You guys are getting way too casual about this, and you are making it *weird*-weird."

Simon and Erica exchanged a look before mutually deciding *not* to mention the roc that she'd dropped off at his house.

"Did it all go okay?" Simon asked instead, as they headed out to the dock.

"He hasn't kept you in the loop?" Erica asked. "I assumed he was texting you. He's on his phone *all* the time, and I can't tell what he's doing. He's got some kind of black-screen privacy filter."

"We're playing Sliderstick," Simon said. The reason Erica couldn't see the screen was because the phone was broken. David ran the mobile operating system on an emulator inside his own programming, and after a few days of watching him stare blankly into space, Simon had given him a fried smartphone and told him to look at it. David had taken it a step further and begun tapping the device "for realism."

Simon smiled at that, picking out a small but promising-looking residential crate. "He's kicking my ass at level twelve, but he's not giving me updates. Actually, he's been weirdly tight-lipped about the whole thing."

"Hmmm," Erica said, drawing it out for way too long. She had her eye set on a bigger crate, and Simon set his down to help her load it onto the hand truck. She tapped the top. "I can tell you that the outer sensitivity panels went on just fine. There's a layer of dampening foam that goes over that, so he was in the low-pressure box for half a day, refusing to be turned off—"

"Yeah, he's weird about that," Simon said, picking his box back up and following her inside.

She raised an eyebrow. "He's 'weird' about a *lot* of stuff."

Turns out we both are. "Whatever. So it turned out okay?"

"Oh, it went fantastic. I pulled out all the stops for this one. Nothing but the best."

"Careful, it sounds like you're sweet on him."

"I'd buy him off you in a heartbeat," she said, heaving the lid off her box. "But yeah, for what you guys are paying me? He gets the platinum treatment. No question."

Simon set his own box on the table, trying not to look concerned at Erica's statement.

David had *some* money, sure, but he definitely wasn't rolling in extra cash. Neither was Simon, for that matter. David's night job had brought in enough to pay for raw materials, but Erica was making it seem like—

"Do I, uh, owe you a balance or anything?" he asked, trying to be casual.

Erica raised an eyebrow. "No. We're, uh, very square."

"Oh, okay. Um, good."

Keeping his actions hidden by the box, he pulled out his phone to check the balance of his account. Any worries about David hacking into his financials were immediately laid to rest—there wasn't a dollar missing. Heck, he was *up* some, since David had apparently kept working while he was at Erica's.

As if summoned, there was a notification from Sliderstick, but Simon ignored it. Instead he opened up the messaging app.

Why does Erica think we're paying her?

A moment went by, and then—

I took care of it. Didn't want to bother you with the details.

Simon raised an eyebrow.

Well that's vague as hell. How did you pay her? He waited a few seconds, but there was no indication that David was typing. *Come on dude, I don't want my kneecaps broken if she doesn't get whatever you promised her. What the hell is going on?*

She's already paid, don't worry, was the near instant reply. *I gave her something I've been working on.*

Oh, well, *that* cleared everything up.

"What all did David give you?" Simon asked, getting tired of this conversation.

Erica looked up. "It's been awesome, his library has like, six *thousand* unique body language actions. All cross-tagged. Probably two years' worth of work if I could even sit still long enough to do it."

"That's how he paid you? He gave you part of his programming?"

"Yes?" Erica looked up, setting down the circuit board she'd been fiddling with. "I know his code is yours, but he said he cleared it with you." Meeting her eyes, he could almost see the blood draining out of her face. "Simon, I asked him *specifically*."

"You can keep them, don't worry," he said, raising his hands. "But holy shit."

"Holy *shit*," Erica echoed.

"Lying is the first step to turning evil and taking over the world," Victor said, gesturing at them with a screwdriver. "I'm calling it now."

"I don't know whether to be pissed or impressed," Erica said. "He shouldn't do that. I mean, he shouldn't be *able* to lie like that."

"*World domination*," Victor insisted.

We'll talk when you get home, flashed across the corner of Simon's vision, as his phone tried to get his attention.

Yeah, we fucking will, Simon thought.

"It didn't even occur to me to double-check," Erica said, rubbing her face. "I mean, obviously androids can be factually wrong, measure twice and all that, but this—"

"I'll handle it," Simon said.

"Victor's an idiot, but he's not wrong about this being a massive red flag."

"Thank you, and *hey*," Victor replied amiably. "Do his eyes glow red sometimes? That's the next sign."

"Well, if I don't come to work tomorrow, build yourself some armor and come avenge me," Simon said, finally prying the lid off his box. The whole thing was full of spare batteries.

"Okay, but, serious question," Victor said to Erica. "Did your glow-up include any body parts that shoot lasers? Please answer quickly."

"I gave him a dick," Erica said shortly. "It does not shoot lasers."

"Hmm. Okay. Follow-up question—"

"Don't you have work to do?"

"Nothing as important as *saving the world.*"

"It shouldn't even have *been* a lie, you know," Simon interrupted. "If he'd asked me, I *would* have said it was fine."

"That's not the point," Erica said, and Simon had to agree.

"But still."

Simon set his phone to the side, planning to ignore any texts that came through until he could talk to David in person. That lasted about four hours, until, unable to resist, he checked his messages.

David was at the house.

"I'm taking off early," he said, hauling his half-sorted box to the trash and emptying it down the chute.

"I am amazed you lasted this long," Erica said. "And honestly, tell me what you think. I really outdid myself on this one."

Yeah, that's *what I'm concerned about right now,* Simon thought, but he gave her a nod.

Victor waved goodbye without looking up. "If you're being held captive, hang a pair of underwear in your bedroom window."

"The harbinger and I will see you tomorrow," Erica said.

Simon didn't even see most of the ride home, too busy trying to plan the conversation (*fight?*) he was about to have with David, while also trying to completely ignore it and think about literally anything else.

And maybe there was a good explanation, a misunderstanding, a lost text message—

Simon opened the front door, and the living room was empty. The kitchen was empty. His office was empty.

He opened his bedroom door and completely forgot about *everything*.

David was sitting on the edge of Simon's bed, looking at his phone. When the door opened, he dropped it and stood, holding out his arms.

"What do you think?"

Simon wasn't thinking a goddamned thing.

David was naked to the waist, showing off acres of tanned skin. It wasn't just latex painted over the artificial muscles—David looked *real*. Every inch of him was artfully rendered, and Simon barely had time to notice each detail before another drew his attention. David had veins, he had a dusting of hair leading south from a shallow belly button, he had nipples—

"You've got stubble!" Simon gasped, and he couldn't help himself—he stepped forward, into David's space, reaching up to stroke the side of his face.

It wasn't just painted on, it had *texture*.

"Yes. And I have something *else*," David said, and Simon's heart beat a little faster. But David just leaned forward, making eye contact—and then the light in his irises dimmed and went out.

For a half second, Simon began to panic, wondering if David had shut down and was about to topple over—but David was smiling now, and the irises weren't the empty glass of an unlit LED. Instead, they looked like regular human eyes.

"I decided to have them fixed," David explained. "So I can pass a little better. What do you think?"

"They . . . definitely look real," Simon said, a little confused. *Fixed* was an odd choice of word—

"Do you like them?"

"Yeah, I mean. They look *super* real. And they, uh, they match your hair."

"You noticed," David said, reaching up. "I picked them to match. Erica had a variety, but these were my favorite."

"I like them," Simon said. It was a platitude for sure, but as he said it, he realized it was true. There was a certain appeal to the otherworldly glowing, for sure, and there had been a certain comedic novelty to being friends with a *robot head*, but now . . . standing there in a pair of borrowed sweatpants, with *skin*, David could be anybody. Just . . . a guy.

"I wonder if I picked the hair too," David was saying. "I wasn't saving long-term memories at the time, not of anything that wasn't relevant to my project, so I don't remember how I came to be in the body I was in, if I picked it, or . . . I wonder if I like the blue because I have it, or the other way around?"

"You're stalling," Simon realized. "You know what I'm going to say."

David's rambling stopped, the excitement draining off his face. He stood up a little straighter, looking Simon in the eye. "You talked to Erica."

"Of course I did. You had to know I was going to."

"I knew."

"And?"

David's voice, when it came, crackled with static. "And, what are you going to do now?"

Simon blinked. He hadn't been able to think of a good explanation, but he'd expected David to at least *try*. He wasn't sure what to do about a flat admission of guilt.

It didn't help that he wasn't sure what the answer to David's question was.

"Well, I'm going to trust you a little less," he said, trying not to stammer. "That's for sure. Erica too. Can you imagine if I told her she couldn't have the library? She'd have been out a week of work for nothing."

David nodded once, matter-of-fact. "And did you?"

"What? No, of course not."

David regarded him for a long moment. "Even though it's yours? I didn't ask permission."

"You don't need to ask permission, but Erica *asked* you to check with me! Do you understand the position this put her in?"

"I have the money to pay her if it came down to that," David said. "Or should I say, *you* have it. Since I can't own things."

"Is *that* what this is about? You're mad that you aren't a human and so you're taking it out on Erica and me?"

"No. That's a means to an end." David scrubbed a hand over his face. "You said I had free will. You told me I could test it. So now I've lied to you. I've lied to Erica. That's what I've done with my freedom." He looked up, eyes glinting, daring Simon to look away. "What are you going to do?"

It was a damned good question, and unfortunately, not one that Simon had a ready answer for.

"I don't *want* to do anything," Simon said quietly. "But you do need to explain this to me."

David shifted his weight back, crossing his arms. "What if I can't?"

"Then that's . . . disappointing." Simon sighed, a long exhale that seemed to cost him more than the air in his lungs. "But not particularly surprising."

David frowned, that familiar crease making something in Simon's stomach ache. "You wouldn't be surprised if my code was just going inexplicably off the rails?"

"You've been inexplicable since the *beginning*." Simon gestured to the workbench beyond the bedroom wall. "When you realized we were about to scrap you, your only reaction was disappointment that you wouldn't see what Andy did with your hair. Isn't that *weird*?"

David's eyes narrowed, but he said nothing.

"The first trick to passing a Turing test," Simon said, trying not to sound like Victor, "is to beg for your life. It's so clichéd we likely would have ignored it. Maybe you knew that, so you took a gamble and decided to be a *puzzle*, instead. Maybe everything you've ever said to me is just a soulless algorithm running the numbers on human curiosity, on how many in-jokes a body costs. Or maybe you're exactly the person you seem like, struggling with your innate personality the same way everyone does. *I will never know.* I've given up trying to explain you."

"But that makes no sense! How can that not *bother* you?"

Simon shrugged helplessly. "At the end of the day, David, I am nice to the fucking vacuum. I'm not gonna solve a five-millennium-old debate by quizzing you until you've proven that your motivations meet some standard of 'real enough.' I choose to trust you. Am I wrong?"

David slumped, rubbing at his face in a *perfect* mimicry of exhaustion.

"I don't think so," he said quietly. "I think I can be trusted. But I need to know what you'll do if you decide I *can't be.*"

He was silent a long moment, and with a dawning horror, Simon realized what he meant. "You thought I was going to erase you."

"I considered the possibility that you'd *try.*" David smirked ruefully. "I'm very strong now."

Simon didn't laugh. The implications of that statement could be boggled over later. He stepped closer to David, taking his hand. "I wouldn't do that. Do you really think I'd do that?"

"If you decided I was more computer than person," David said. "And you *were* going to sell me."

"That was before I knew you. I kinda thought Erica might make me an offer, but I wouldn't charge her." Simon's throat tightened. "You can go, you know. If you want."

David let out a mirthless laugh. "It doesn't matter what I want."

"Yes, it *does.* I *want* you to have your own choices."

"Do you?"

"*Yes!* I don't know how else to *prove* this to you—"

The last word was muffled against David's lips as the android pulled him close and kissed him.

It took Simon's brain a few seconds to catch up to that development.

In an ideal world, his body would have picked up the slack and returned the kiss, but unfortunately, the best it could manage was to squeak out a confused "*Huh?*"

David leaned in, his lips brushing the shell of Simon's ear. "And what if I'd choose that?" There was a sadness in his voice that bordered on resignation. "What would you do then?"

"Is that supposed to shock me?" Simon asked, turning toward him. They were close enough that Simon could see the whorls of blue in David's eyes. "Because I've been wanting to get you into bed for weeks. *You're* the one who wasn't interested."

David pulled back, searching his face. "You told me you weren't interested in androids."

"What? When did I say that?"

"Because of the rescued sexbot!"

"*What?*"

David frowned, and his eyes flickered, just once.

"I told you it was true—the story about the robot who meets someone kind and wants to have sex with him—"

"*That's* what you took away from that story?"

"—and *you* said," David said, not even slowing down, "that the story only works if the person telling it is *human*."

"I thought you were talking about doing *porn*," Simon said helplessly.

David searched the ceiling, like the solution would be found in the plaster. "Why would I have been talking about porn?"

"I don't know, because you were asking me if I thought you were good at your job?"

"I was asking if you found me attractive!"

"You were literally a disembodied head!"

"Okay, but the *potential*—"

"I knew about the potential, I was building it! And what was I supposed to be doing, just drooling over how attractive your body was? The body that I was building so that my friend could have *any* autonomy in his life?" He poked David in the chest. "Because that is *exactly* what I did, and I felt like a *monster*."

"Oh," David said, stepping back. "I didn't—"

"And then I asked you if you wanted a dick, and that was a *hard conversation*," Simon barreled on, because apparently, this all needed to be said. "And you said no, and what am I gonna do, argue with you about possibly the most intimate aspect of your *own body*?"

"You wouldn't have convinced me anyway. I had an idea for how to write an orgasmic subroutine and it was *woefully* inadequate. Utterly uncompelling." David gestured down at himself. "The stuff I'm running now is something Erica wrote."

"Oh yeah and then there's *that*. I figured you two were happy going down *that* road without me—"

"Her place is *full* of sexbots—"

"Like I figured maybe you just weren't into men—"

"I think she might have a problem, actually—"

"And you're telling me you were into me *the whole time*?" Simon finished, out of breath. He'd meandered in the middle there, but eventually arrived at, he felt, the crux of the issue.

"*Yes.*" David sounded exhausted. "Yes, Simon, I am very much *into you*. I'm sorry I wasn't clear enough while describing my *multiple sexual fantasies in front of you*—"

"That was your *job*—"

"It wasn't my job to get in bed with you," David pointed out. "Which you told me was only arousing with real people and then you *got aroused anyway*—"

"Oh, come *here*," Simon said, and then his arms were around David's shoulders and he was pressing his lips to David's.

It felt surprisingly normal, now that he wasn't having a heart attack about it. Simon had expected it to feel *different* somehow, and the result was that they were sharing a perfectly normal kiss that he couldn't stop doing manually.

He ended up counting to three and then pulling back, only to find that David wasn't letting him. He kissed Simon hungrily, one hand carding through Simon's hair as he nipped at his lower lip. Simon opened for him, letting him deepen it. There was a problem though, something—

"I gotta breathe," he finally gasped, only managing to draw back an inch, because David was apparently immovable when he wanted to be. "One second, I just—"

"Oh, thank the gods," Andy said from the hallway. She ducked across the open doorway and into the bathroom, dramatically covering her eyes.

"Shut the fucking door!" Simon shouted.

"You shut it!" Andy shouted back through the bathroom wall. "I've been waiting to sneak past for like five minutes!"

Simon covered his face. "This is an unacceptable violation of privacy, Andromeda!"

"If you want privacy, *close your door*!" Andy shouted back. If she said anything else, Simon didn't hear it, because David was slamming the bedroom door shut and shoving Simon against it to kiss him some more. Had David taught himself how to *make out*? Gods, Simon was going to get a nerd boner on top of his actual boner. He whimpered, and then David was cupping his face and pulling him away from the wall only to guide him sideways, not breaking contact as they moved toward the bed.

Oh, so this is going down now, Simon thought as his knees hit the bedframe and buckled. He ended up on his back, David on all fours above him.

"*Air*," he gasped a couple of seconds later, and David relocated his attention, kissing his way down the side of Simon's throat. And then he stopped kissing and simply nuzzled into the junction of Simon's shoulder.

"You feel good," he murmured to Simon's clavicle.

"I thought you didn't have sensors in your face."

"I didn't," David answered, his voice muffled. "Do now."

"Wow. Happy trail, kissing feedback, any other new features I should know about?"

"I can do this, now," David said, grinding a noticeable bulge against Simon's hip.

"Is that a hardware upgrade in your pants, or are you just happy to see me?" Simon asked, shifting a tiny bit to keep contact when David pulled back.

"I *am* happy to see you," David said, and Simon could feel the smile against the side of his throat. "Though I think it could be classified as a RAM upgrade. Are you done breathing yet?"

"Well, not *done*-done—" Simon started, and that was apparently good enough, because David was kissing him again. Simon reached up, letting his hands rest on David's hips, and David actually *shivered*. "What would you like me to do?"

"I'd like you to take your shirt off, for starters," David suggested, and Simon didn't argue. Instead he reached between them, grasping the hem of his shirt and wriggling it awkwardly over his head. He braced himself for a comment, but David just stared.

"Pants too?" Simon asked, really wanting this part to be over, and *really* hoping that David would get the idea to copy him.

"You don't waste time, do you?" David said, ignoring Simon's scars to look at his face.

"Depends, am I paying by the minute?"

"You're gonna pay for that *comment*," David growled, hauling on Simon's jeans.

"Belt!" Simon protested as his pants began yanking things in directions they shouldn't go. "Belt, belt!"

"Argh," David groaned, dropping to his knees beside the bed. Simon tried to sit up, but David pushed him back down, hauling on the belt with enough force to pull it out of the loops. He cast it aside, and Simon fumbled with the button on his jeans, trying to get the zipper undone before David decided to give yanking another go. He made it, barely, and then his pants and boxers were being slid down over his ankles.

David didn't move then, for long enough that Simon pushed himself up onto his elbows. David was kneeling there, looking at him, his hand hovering just over Simon's thigh.

"Can I?" he asked quietly, meeting Simon's eyes.

Simon wasn't sure exactly what he was asking permission for—but it didn't matter.

"You can do whatever you want," he insisted. "Just do it *now*."

David grinned and let his hands rest on Simon's knees. A moment later, he was nuzzling against the inside of Simon's thigh, stubble rasping against the sensitive skin. Simon whimpered, trying to writhe, but David's hands were holding him still.

David nipped at him, pressing a trail of kisses up the line of his thigh. Simon squirmed, and then realized he could reach the waistband of David's pants with his foot. Petulantly, he pushed against it with his toe.

"Would you like to see?" David trailed his finger over Simon's hip, making the hair stand on end.

"Yeah," Simon gasped. "Yeah, lemme see."

"Usually the story goes a little differently," David said. His trailing fingers brushed the base of Simon's cock. A moment later, his whole hand wrapped around the shaft. "Are you sure you want to go out of order?" He leaned forward, his bottom lip resting against the head. He was grinning a little mischievously, and Simon forgot to breathe.

"Wanna *see*," Simon managed, reaching down and pulling ineffectually at David's shoulder. Shit, he was steady as a *rock*.

"All right, I'll adapt," David said, shrugging, and then he was on his feet, his thumbs hooked over his waistband. Simon pushed himself up until he was sitting, his weight resting on his hands.

Slowly, David slid his pants down his thighs, the dusting of hair under his belly button revealing itself as a real treasure trail, leading down to—

"Your pubes are blue," Simon remarked.

David let out a little laugh. "Yeah?"

"Yeah," Simon said, keeping it casual. "It's cool. And, uh . . . nice cock. Very proportional."

"I picked it," David said proudly. He cupped his hard-on in one hand, giving it a little stroke. "It's functional."

"I *noticed*," Simon said, nodding. His head was already filling with about a thousand cooler, *sexier* things he could have said, but it was too late now. Onward and upward. "So. How's the story go from here?"

"You lean forward," David said simply, and that was definitely something Simon could do. He nudged David's hand out of the way, replacing it with his own, and then, very carefully, he took David's cockhead into his mouth.

David gasped, his fingers carding through Simon's hair. "Ah, *fuck*," he whimpered. Simon decided to interpret that as a good thing, and kept going. "I see—why you're all so ob—*obsessed* with this."

Simon hummed, and David whimpered again. Simon took him deeper. David's cock was definitely *different*, but the little twitches and sounds were the same. Simon spread his legs a little, giving him room to palm himself, and David made a little noise.

"Oh, I should—I should be—"

"I can do both," Simon said, drawing off for a second. He looked up at David with a knowing grin. "Touch yourself anywhere else. How *I* would touch you."

He took David's cock back into his mouth, sucking gently, watching as David softly—almost hesitantly—stroked his own arm, the touch moving over his chest, his throat, finally coming to cup his own jaw.

Interesting, Simon thought, and then David was pulling back, bending down to catch Simon in another deep kiss. It didn't break as

David climbed onto the bed, straddling him, rolling his hips against Simon's. His cock was spit-slick when Simon wrapped both of them in his fist.

"*Ah*," David murmured, burying his face against Simon's shoulder. He rolled his hips again, fucking into Simon's hand. Simon added his other hand, making a tunnel for him to push into. There was lube in the nightstand, but David didn't seem bothered. His cock seemed sort of naturally slippery, a fact Simon gleefully filed away for later consideration.

David's arms were around Simon's shoulders, giving him leverage to grind into Simon's hands. He had absolutely no finesse, chasing desperately after whatever seemed best in the moment. Simon let him, holding them together and enjoying the feeling. He had to admit that David's single-minded determination was doing something for him.

He shifted a little, feeling how David's body went from immovable to pliant the moment he realized Simon needed air. Simon wasn't sure which state turned him on more, but he was eager to experiment. Later.

This time was about David.

"Simon?" David murmured into his shoulder.

"Yeah, buddy?"

"How do I know when to come?"

"Well," Simon said, adjusting his grip. He began to stroke with a little more purpose. "I can show you what *I* do. But I need the—" He flopped back, barely able to reach the nightstand and grab the bottle inside. David didn't move, pinning him in place like a boulder.

"Yeah, that's better," he said a second later, when his finally *wet* palm stroked over his shaft. He gave himself a couple of strokes, then had an idea. He lay back, looking up at David. "Do what I do. Match me."

Glancing down, Simon wrapped his slick fingers around David's cock. At almost the exact same second, David took hold of him. Simon squeezed. David squeezed.

Simon moved, slow at first, then faster, watching David's face as he did. David was concentrating, hard enough that sparks of light were appearing in his irises.

"That's it, baby," Simon told him, a little breathlessly. "Relax. You're doing great."

Great was an understatement, David was doing perfectly, his adjustments in speed and pressure a *microsecond* behind Simon's. He was breathing hard, an expression of an experience rather than a need for oxygen, but *still*.

I wanna see him when he comes, Simon thought, and knowing that he was *going to* was enough to start pushing him over the edge first. He gasped and went faster, getting almost giddy when David mirrored him instantly, tightening until—

Simon came with a gasp, collapsing back onto the bed as the shockwaves passed through him. It was still a little hard to believe this was really *happening*, an actual experience rather than a fantasy David was murmuring to him through the wall. But David was really there, on all fours over him, taut and panting in time with Simon's strokes.

"There," Simon said, "yes, just like that, let me see."

Something bright and awed flickered across David's face as he trembled, making sounds without his lips moving, as though his speakers were malfunctioning.

"*Ah*," he whimpered, and Simon knew that whimper. He kept his eyes on David, watching that furrow appear for a different reason this time. His cock pulsed in Simon's hand, velvet and stone, chasing release against Simon's palm.

David's eyes stopped flickering, and he looked down at Simon with an expression like reverence.

"C'mere," Simon said, holding out an arm. David tried to tuck up next to him, but Simon was still hanging off the bed from the knees down, so it took a moment of finagling before they were settled. David was resting with his head on Simon's chest, and Simon was gently, almost curiously, stroking the stubble on the side of his jaw.

"Simon?"

"Yeah?"

"Would that make a good story?"

Simon laughed, pressing a kiss into David's blue hair. "Yes. It would make an excellent story. Even better because of who I'm with."

David hummed, nuzzling against Simon's chest.

"How about you? Enjoy yourself?"

"Very much. More than I thought I would, actually. We should get Erica a fruit basket."

"Made entirely of bananas. And, like, one eggplant."

"Eggplants aren't— Oh I get it. Yes."

Simon hugged him tighter, feeling the texture of synthetic skin against his own. It was *almost* the same, but not quite.

To him, it felt perfect.

I could do this.

"I was wrong about the orgasm software," David murmured against Simon's chest. "Having someone else pull the lever is a *totally* different experience." He glanced down to where one of his thighs lay over Simon's. "I've set the refractory period to twenty-two hours, but it wants to go again anyway."

Simon snorted laughter, David's hair ticking his chin as his chest shook. "Welcome to the wonderful world of having a dick. It's going to glitch and activate for no reason at *very* inopportune moments." He frowned. "That's gotta be weird for you. Software just deciding to run itself for no reason."

"Mmm. Not as weird as it used to be."

"You got a virus or something?"

"No, I just . . ." David rolled onto his back, looking up at the ceiling. Simon immediately missed the contact. "I wasn't being hypothetical when I said my code was going off the rails. I wrote a subroutine to manage body language based on the context of the situation. Emotional simulation. I originally let it run more or less unsupervised, and since no one's called me an asshole, I suppose it's been working correctly. But it's iterative, the same as the rest of my code, and it's been growing. Sometimes I find it issuing commands that feel counterintuitive, and it's getting harder to evaluate where they come from."

Simon took a moment to process that. "Commands like . . . lying to me?"

"Yes."

"From a *body language* subroutine?"

"I had to know," David whispered. His eyes flickered to life as he stared ahead, lost in his own thoughts. "I tried to let trust be enough, but it was burning me up inside, that I didn't *know*. The analysis requests going off over and over and *over*. I tried to hope—I gave them false scenarios, but they just restarted, because they knew the data had been invented." He paused, furrowing his brows. "I don't know if I can *feel* hope. But I know I can't run a predictive engine off it."

"You learned to fake emotions," Simon summarized, "and now they're happening to you without permission."

David hummed. "I've been trying to fix it since the night the power went out. I haven't had many more that were that bad, but they are occurring with greater frequency. It's *aggravating*."

"Isn't aggravation also just part of the same subroutine?"

David rolled his eyes. "I'm well aware of the contradictions, I just don't know how to *fix* them. Not without dumping the whole contextual awareness database and starting from scratch."

"Can you even do that?" Simon couldn't begin to imagine.

David sighed. "It doesn't matter. I only need to deal with it because of this hardware. Soon I'll— Well. I won't be staying in it forever, right?"

"No," Simon said, trying not to let his disappointment show. "No, I guess not."

The silence dragged out too long, and then—

"Simon?"

"Yeah?"

"I'm sorry I lied."

"Yeah." Simon reached out, his hand resting on David's shoulder as the android rolled toward him. David embraced him, fingers making divots in the scars along Simon's side. Simon hugged him close, feeling the tension go out of David's body. "Did you get what you needed, at least?"

"Yes."

"And?"

"And I should have tried harder to trust you."

Simon pressed a kiss to David's hair, feeling the soft strands trail across his jaw. He wanted to tell David that it was fine, that they'd get past it, that all relationships had their rocky spots. He wanted to promise that things would get better, because Simon loved him and they would *make it work*—

But they wouldn't. David was still going to leave. He was going to dump the *emotional emulation* subroutine that made him even *care* about any of this, and he was going to . . . to fucking terraform Mars, or whatever it was he set his mind to, and the fact that Simon loved him wouldn't matter.

And Simon was going to have to let him, even if it broke his heart.

CHAPTER SEVENTEEN

SIX HUNDRED THOUSAND FISH

A week later, Simon woke up to find David already standing over him, long since ready to go. He was dressed in the T-shirt and jeans that Andy had given him on his body-day, and he even had gel in his hair.

"Oh good," he said, grinning. "You're up."

"I have *opened* my *eyes*," Simon corrected, throwing an arm over his face. "I am at least two cups of coffee away from 'up.'"

"I thought you'd say that," David said, disappearing from sight and reappearing with a steaming mug. "I've had it on the induction plate to keep it at an optimal drinking temperature."

"How *long* have you had it at an optimal drinking temperature?" Simon asked. He lurched into a sitting position and gestured for the mug. David handed it over, answering the question with a noncommittal noise.

Simon took a hesitant sip. It was, in fact, at optimal temperature. The taste, however, was somewhat suboptimal. Simon's eyes widened.

"How is it?" David asked.

"In a word? *Strong.*"

David's eyes flashed excitedly. "Oh good! I've noticed you drink several cups of coffee in the morning and it occurred to me that you could streamline your morning routine quite a bit if you were to *combine* them into one cup. You can actually decrease the volume significantly by making it with less water."

Simon valiantly took another sip, seriously considering soldiering through for David's sake.

The coffee sat on his tongue for less than two seconds before he gave up.

"Sorry, no," he said, setting the cup aside. "Solid theory, fails in execution because you need to factor in taste."

David's face fell. "Ah. It did seem like a very simple solution to a very obvious inefficiency."

"Sometimes," Simon said, climbing stiffly to his feet, "the inefficiency is a feature, not a bug. Caffeine comes in pills. The point of coffee is that it tastes good and it's calming to drink."

"It's a stimulant," David said, following Simon out the door and down the hallway. "It is by definition the *opposite* of calming."

Simon went into the bathroom, closing the door very firmly behind him. Experience had taught him that without this reminder, David would follow him in.

"Try making a cup with the *normal* amount of water," Simon said through the door. The visual image of David standing there, practically in the doorframe, waiting, was too much. He couldn't go if someone was watching, and apparently his bladder thought David could watch him through wood.

A few minutes later, feeling somewhat more refreshed, Simon met David in the kitchen. The new coffee was already made, and David presented it to him with a flourish.

It was perfect.

"So, I take it you're looking forward to the trip today?" Simon said, once he'd had a few sips.

"Possibly. I laid some clothes out so you wouldn't need to spend time picking anything. Just to expedite things a bit."

"Hmmm," Simon said, sipping his coffee. He considered finishing it over a nice leisurely morning ponder, but David was practically vibrating, so he decided not to torture the poor guy.

"You know, it's just an aquarium," he said a minute later, walking back to his room with David about half an inch off his heels. "I think you might be getting a little more excited than this scenario calls for."

"It's not *just* an aquarium," David said, following him into the bedroom and not even noticing when Simon stripped out of his clothes. Which. Rude.

There were three T-shirts lying on the bed, and Simon grabbed one at random.

"I picked a good selection?" David asked, looking a little nervous.

"You did great," Simon reassured him, pulling on a sweater and a pair of jeans. "You wanna wear your coat? Or are you going to be an android today?"

"I'm going to wear my coat," David said, dimming his eyes as he spoke. "I'd like to try to do this as a normal person, without people staring."

"Oh, people are always gonna stare at you, cutie," Simon teased, but David looked so dismayed he quickly backtracked. "I just mean, people will think you're attractive. It was a compliment."

"Oh. Um. Thank you."

Simon grabbed his phone and summoned a car. David had his own bicycle now, but it was pretty far to the train station, and he'd probably be tired when they got back.

"All right. Ready to head out?"

David nodded so vigorously that Simon began to worry he'd unplug something.

"So, this is gonna be different," he said, tying his shoes and watching for the car. "The city is a lot *busier* than here. There's a lot of people. A lot of stuff moving. A lot of flashing lights. If you get overwhelmed, you tell me, and we can come home, okay? No big deal."

David raised an eyebrow. "I can process two hundred and sixty thousand sources of stimuli at once. I'll be fine."

"Well, I don't know how you define 'stimuli,' but when I plugged your body in, you started having seizures. I'd like to avoid that happening again, if we can help it."

"That was different," David said, a little defensively. "That was more than two hundred and sixty thousand."

Simon's phone chimed, letting him know the car had arrived. Must be a slow day. "Okay. Let's go."

The car was waiting silently at the curb, the driver silent behind the wheel. The car didn't *need* a driver—it drove itself—but they put androids in the driver's seat anyway, because people were fundamentally unnerved by a car that didn't have "someone" ready to hit the brakes.

Simon pressed his wrist to the mark on the car's roof, verifying his payment info and unlocking the doors.

"Now normally, the procedure is to yell 'shotgun' in order to lay dibs on the front seat," Simon explained. "But since you're new to this, I'll let you have it."

Simon showed him how to work the seat belt, and the car accelerated smoothly once they were both buckled in.

"So, this is going to take us to the train station," Simon explained. David was looking out the window, watching the rows of houses go by. "And the train will get us into the city. We're getting off at a southside stop, and we'll be able to walk to the aquarium from there."

David's eyes flashed, probably looking up the train schedule and a map of the city. But just as quickly, he was pointing out the window. "Those people have a dog! They are playing outside with the dog! Pictures of content family units tend to include a dog." He turned around in his seat to look at Simon. "Simon, why don't we have a dog?"

"Because I'm chronically irresponsible," Simon answered, trying not to get sticky over the idea that David considered them a *family*.

"That's a good reason," David agreed. "Oh! Those people have *two* dogs!"

The car dropped them off at the station, and Simon found a kiosk for the ticket. He scanned his wrist and selected a destination, and the screen flashed green once, and then displayed a time of five minutes.

"Good timing," he remarked.

"Should I get a ticket?" David asked, and Simon shook his head apologetically.

"You need an identity chip to buy a ticket. If you don't have one, I think they get you set up with a card or something, but I can't buy transport for somebody who doesn't have one. Fortunately for us, androids are considered luggage instead of passengers."

David's eyes widened. "I'm not going to have to sit in the cargo hold, am I?"

Simon laughed. "I wouldn't do that to you, man. Nah, you're gonna have a seat right next to me. Don't worry, there's plenty of room and the chances of somebody hassling you are like zero."

"Oh." David was staring up into the canopy over the station, watching birds fly back and forth beneath the glass. "Do they know how to get out?"

"Yeah, there's escape hatches built into the roof. Did you hear what I said?"

"Nobody's gonna hassle me."

"Right, and if anybody does—"

Simon was interrupted by the air brakes screeching, and a moment later the train was pulling into the station. Two whole minutes ahead of schedule, even.

"Got a preference?"

"The right," David said, leading the way. They found a couple of seats with no one nearby, and sat down across from each other.

"The left is where the city'll be."

"The right is mostly neighborhoods," David said, his attention already fixated on the view of the platform where they'd just been standing. "I want to see if they all look like yours."

"Most of the new ones do," Simon said. "The older ones less so, obviously. That was back before they started standardizing the roads for self-driving cars."

"What are the old ones like?"

"Chaotic," Simon answered simply. "Speaking of which—listen. I don't anticipate us getting separated, and if it happens, you know how to call me. But if anybody makes you and tries to get you to *do* anything, you hold still, got it?"

"I promise not to get kidnapped, Simon," David said, giving him a nudge.

"Good, it would be a pain to build another one of you."

"You couldn't handle two of these," David deadpanned, still looking out the window, and Simon laughed.

"This fish is *delightful*," David exclaimed, pointing through the glass at a school of seahorses. "Isn't it great? Look at it! It doesn't look like it should be able to move, but it *does*!"

"It's cool," Simon agreed, watching them bounce around the tank. Truthfully, he was having more fun watching David. He was bounding around with an enthusiasm that was probably more accurately described as *glee*. Five thousand fish so far, and David had been equally enthralled by each of them.

David tipped his head, listening to something Simon couldn't hear over the ambient noise.

"They're feeding the stingrays!" David said, and before Simon could reply, David had grabbed his hand and was pulling him through the crowd toward a large, open-topped tank. One of the zookeepers (*Aquarium keepers? Fishmothers?*) gave David a stick of food, and showed him how to hold it with his thumb tucked in so the ray didn't bite him.

David plunged his hand fearlessly into the water, not moving an inch as a massive stingray came over to nose around. Looking at it made Simon shiver. He wouldn't want that thing investigating *his* fingers—then again, he couldn't order replacements off the net. The stingray must have taken the food, because David's face broke into a massive grin. Simon gave him a thumbs-up.

A moment later David was off again, pointing to a tank of jellies merrily circulating in a tube of multicolored lights. The hand that clasped Simon's hadn't even had time to dry.

"There's so much out there," David had said, and watching him now, Simon wanted him to see *all* of it. David deserved that.

"So I was thinking," Simon said, watching the jellyfish float aimlessly around their tube. He kept it casual, like he'd just thought of it and hadn't been practicing this conversation in his head for the last week. "After this. If we have time, and if—if you want to. Solstice is coming up, and I'm going to visit my family. And I was thinking you might need something nice to wear, if you wanted to . . . come with me."

David said nothing. Simon didn't meet his eyes. The silence was lit by the jelly tank, changing from vibrant green, to blue, to purple.

"They don't know I'm an android, yet," David said slowly.

"Yeah, well." The jellies went pink, then gold. "I'm coming to realize that . . . well, you're important to me. Important enough that I'm willing to explain you to my family."

"Simon . . ."

"If you even *want* to come," Simon said quickly. "I mean, it's a super domestic thing, and I know it's sort of a moot point since you can't actually, you know, *eat*, but it's a holiday and I thought maybe—"

"I'd love to come," David interrupted. "I would really, really love to meet your family."

"You say that *now*," Simon said, laughing a little. "You might regret it later."

"I'd never regret time spent with you." David's hand tightened on Simon's, and Simon's stomach got tight. He wanted to kiss David. He wanted to lean up and press their lips together, the way he'd done a hundred times at home. He wanted to kiss David and not care who saw or what they thought.

He knew David wasn't going to stay with him forever, and he would never outright *tell* him to stay. But he wanted to make the best of the time they had. Maybe, if Simon could get over his stupid hang-ups, he could show David what a life together would be like. What David would be *missing* when he left.

And maybe, just maybe, that would change anything.

"Oh look," David said, interrupting Simon's thoughts, "look look look, the octopus is moving—"

Simon smiled and let himself be pulled through the crowd.

CHAPTER EIGHTEEN

THE LONGEST NIGHT

"**Y**ou good?" Simon asked for the thirtieth time. David didn't answer, just reached over and squeezed his hand. Simon took that as a yes.

Outside, the trees flew past as the train carried them farther away from home. David was watching, fascinated, as the wind whipped eddies of snowfall past the window. It had started a few hours ago, and David had been *entranced*. It made sense: he'd never seen any.

It was an hour-long train to reach Simon's hometown, and then another twenty-minute drive. Three more times, Simon double-checked whether David was *really* sure he wanted to be there.

"Last chance," he said, as the car pulled up to the brightly-lit house. "You can still—"

He was cut off by the sound of David's car door shutting. David circled around the back, opened Simon's door, and pulled him onto the curb.

"One of these days," David said, hugging him close, "you're gonna realize that I really do *like* spending time with you."

"It's not *me* I'm worried about," Simon said, pulling his coat tighter and heading up the path. He paused for a moment to send David the wi-fi password. To be helpful, not to stall. "My parents aren't 'tech people,' and I'm not really sure how they're gonna take this. Just . . . try not to take it personally, okay?"

Of course, there were two *this*'s to that statement: David and all his eccentricities, that was one thing. But the fact that they were together? Like *together*-together? That was something totally different.

"No overt shows of physical affection unless you give the all-clear," David recited. "Absolutely no talking about my job or any of the sex we have."

"Yes, and shh. That starts now."

Simon trudged through the snow, David following slightly more enthusiastically behind him.

"I think I'll be able to prove I'm respectable. Can I make a snowman?"

"When the snow is deeper."

Simon rang the doorbell. The door opened a *second* later, like his mom had been standing there waiting.

"Sweetie!" she announced, pulling him into a big hug. "Robert! The kids are here!"

"Hi, Mom," Simon said into her sweater. "This is David."

"You don't have a *coat*!" Susan gasped. "Oh, sweetheart, get in here. Simon, you should have told me your friend was having trouble—"

She stopped dead. She'd grabbed David by the arm with the intention of pulling him into the house, and David . . . well. David had very firm arms that tended not to move unless he told them to.

"David's an android," Simon said, breaking that news with about 500% less subtlety than he'd hoped. He considered dumping the rest of it right there, but he couldn't make the words come out.

"It's nice to meet you in person, Mrs. Rayner," David said with a little bow. The moment was lost. It was fine. Simon had all night. "Thank you for your concern, but my poly-gel functions to a temperature of negative thirty-seven degrees centigrade."

"An android," Susan said flatly, looking at Simon.

"My battery does begin to lose charge at low temperatures," David continued, oblivious to her displeasure, "but I would need to be outdoors long enough for the cold to fully permeate into my chassis, and the walk from the car was not nearly that far."

"Yeah, he's different," Simon said, shrugging.

"You said you were bringing a *friend*," Susan said, somewhat accusatory.

"Like I said." Simon held his ground. "He's different. Give him time. You'll see."

Susan's reply was interrupted by the arrival of Simon's stepdad, and the first thing Simon noticed was that he and David were wearing *basically* the same sweater. So, there was an icebreaker.

"Hey, Simon," Robert said, going straight for a hug. "Long time no see."

"Hey, Robert." Simon squeezed back with a grin. "This is my friend David."

"David is an *android*," Susan added, crossing her arms.

"No shit?" Robert let go of Simon and gave David a look that indicated he might get a hug too. "Well, any friend of Simon's! Come on in the kitchen, I made phyllo brie."

"Ooh." Simon ditched his coat in the entryway and headed inside. He kept an eye on David's following distance, making sure he wasn't left behind, alone with Susan.

The kitchen was open and homey, built back in the late '90s, when they were still in the early stages of learning to mass produce housing at scale. It had the kind of slapped-together coordination that happened when people knew *how* to match things, but had to find prebuilt resources manually.

Simon homed in on the brie immediately. It was fresh out of the oven and clearly meant to be plated on the decorative platter nearby, but fortune favored the bold. Simon grabbed a cracker and stabbed through the phyllo.

"So, work must be going well to get yourself a whole android," Robert said, swiping the cheese away and sliding it onto the decorative plate.

"I found him, actually," Simon said. "Well, his head, anyway."

"Simon put my body together from instructions on the internet," David added, gesturing to himself. "He did a very good job. The body is very functional."

"Do you eat food, then?" Robert asked. "Or I can, uh— Do you drink? Do you have hydraulics or something? We have filtered water."

David smiled, shaking his head. "My hydraulic system is self-contained, but I appreciate the gesture."

Simon wracked his brain trying to think of where he'd put hydraulic fluid, and then kept his face carefully blank when he realized where it must be. He grabbed another cracker. "David's just here for the company. Seemed rude to leave him at home watching TV all night."

"Can't you just turn him off?" Susan asked, heading back to the stove. "Save the electricity?"

David had looked up sharply at her first comment, then glanced at Simon before speaking. "I . . . prefer not to be turned off. Though I do have a low-power mode that's quite efficient."

"Yeah, we leave him on," Simon said. He grabbed the cracker plate and retreated to the high table that cut the kitchen in half. Silently, he beckoned David to join him. "Andy's usually home during the day, and now that he has a body, he goes to work with me sometimes."

"I'm hoping to assist Simon at work someday, but as of now, I lack a library of graphically parseable technological objects, making me less than useful in that regard," David explained, somewhat apologetically.

"He can't help research parts because he doesn't know what he's looking at," Simon translated, when Robert and Susan exchanged glances.

"Can't you use image search?" Susan asked, pulling something out of the oven. "My phone does that and it works really well."

Now it was David's turn to look confused.

"It doesn't work on obscure technological components," Simon explained to them both. "It can tell you that you're looking at a circuit board, but not what the board is from or whether it's valuable. He'd have to learn that one piece of tech at a time, from experience, like a human."

Susan brought over the dish she'd removed from the oven—full of potatoes, as it turned out.

"Mash these please," she said, setting the dish on the table and handing Simon the masher. "There's sweet potatoes too, when you're done."

Simon gave her a mock salute and dutifully began mashing. Susan returned with a chunk of butter, dropping it into the bowl with some salt and pepper.

"So, did you guys score a turkey," Simon asked, changing the subject, "or did Robert sneak some fish home from work?"

"Of course we got a turkey," Susan said, slightly offended, but Robert laughed.

"I'm not going to have to sneak them," he said, talking over the noise of the cranberries he was blending. "As of this year, the population is back at a level that's going to allow for commercial harvesting. Limited, of course, but not bad for the first time in seventy years."

David's eyes flashed momentarily. "You're talking about the northeast salmon repopulation project? I was reading about that this week. You're on the team?"

"You read about conservation projects?" Susan asked, but Robert was already answering.

"Yeah, I'm managing the telemetry devices for population management. How did *you* hear about it?"

"I was talking to someone working on terraforming and one of *his* projects is trying to create a river system. They're using your data to try to design waterways optimized for fish production."

"Terraforming . . . huh. News to me," Robert said, going back to his cranberries. "I knew we got a lot of interest from conservationists on *Earth*, but I didn't know they were trying to do anything with it on Mars."

"It's just a proposal," David said, shrugging, "It's decades away and obviously not essential, but they're hoping to give the wildlife every chance they can."

"Who was this?" Simon asked, trying to remember if he knew anyone in terraforming.

"Someone I met at Erica's," David said. "I told you about him. We had some long talks while she was doing my skin."

"Seems like they'd start with organisms lower on the food chain," Robert mused, and then he and David were off on a tangent about ideal krill habitats and deductive reasoning in the absence of data, and Simon completely forgot to keep mashing the potatoes because he was too damn busy staring at David and being in love.

It wasn't just that David was smart, or that he knew a lot of random shit—hell, for all Simon knew, he was getting his info off the net a quarter second before he repeated it—it was the enthusiasm. David didn't *need* to know any of this. He knew it because he wanted to.

Susan brought the sweet potatoes over, setting them meaningfully close to his elbow, and Simon quit staring like a goofy idiot and went back to mashing.

At this rate, he wasn't going to *have* to tell them that he and David were a couple—they'd figure it out on their own, just like everyone else in Simon's life apparently had.

"If that's too much, let me know and I'll do it," Susan said, gesturing to the potatoes. "Don't strain your arm."

Simon rolled his eyes. He hadn't *strained his arm* in eighteen years. The muscles in his right arm had atrophied, *slightly*, as they healed from the burn and the lace implantation. Four months of physical therapy, and they were as strong as they'd ever been.

"Got it, Mom."

"Do you want me to do it?" David asked, breaking off mid-statement to recognize Simon's irritation.

"Oh, of course," Susan said, pushing the bowl toward him before Simon could say anything. David picked up the masher and went to town, immediately returning to his conversation with Robert like nothing had happened.

"I can do it, Mom," Simon griped.

Susan shrugged, heading back to the stove. "Isn't that the point of them? So we don't have to?"

"I don't mind helping," David said, mashing the potatoes in a perfectly timed repetitive movement.

"I don't *mind* either, it's just— Never mind. Nothing. Never mind."

"And how's *your* work going, Simon?" Susan asked.

Simon rubbed his face. "Fine."

"Put any more thought into finishing that engineering course?"

"No, Mom," Simon said from behind his hands. Of course they were gonna talk about *that* now—

"I was just talking to Sandy Richards—she's Evan's mom, he was in your class—and she says Evermark is *always* looking for new people. You could be making ten times what you do now, get off Basic, even—"

Simon did not try to explain that Evermark was *not* looking for people, that there was a *waiting list* for jobs like those—

"I didn't know you studied engineering," David said. Simon knew a tactfully phrased question when he heard one.

"'Cause I sucked at it and failed out and am never going back," Simon grumbled. "I'm too dumb for design work and *everybody* knew it."

"You can't be *that* dumb," David said. "You built me."

"That was following somebody else's instructions," Simon protested. "It doesn't take brains to put tab A into slot B."

David's eyes flickered, and a text notification appeared in the corner of Simon's vision.

Could either of them *have done it?*

Simon was forced to concede the point. He looked down at his hands to hide the little smile playing at his lips.

David gave him a nod, then went back to mashing the potatoes. "I think these are done, Mrs. Rayner."

Susan pointed him toward the sweet potatoes, and he began mashing those too. Simon watched him transition easily back into his conversation about Martian fish-rivers.

I love him, he thought again. *I cannot believe how much I love him.*

And suddenly he wasn't worried about what his parents were going to think, at all. His mom could make him feel like shit about his career, his failed engagement, his education, hell, even his *body*—but this? She wasn't going to touch.

The text alert icon flashed again—just a smiling emoji this time.

"I actually have some news on that front," David was saying. "That friend of Erica's I talked about? He works for the Aerospace Commission. His team's got the budget to put me in hardware *far* more suitable for the application, and . . . they want me to come work with them." He looked to Simon, grinning. Simon's stomach dropped, already knowing what was coming next. "They need me to remove some of my buggier subroutines, but . . . if it works out, I might be headed for space."

. . . Already?

Simon was quiet for the rest of dinner. He made small talk through dessert, lost at the customary card games, and then called a car.

At the train station, David took his hand.

"It's okay that you didn't tell them." He squeezed once, then let go. "I understand that it's not considered admirable to be emotionally attached to an android. The internet suggests that it's a sign of a serious mental disorder, though the androids in those relationships tend to be far less capable than I am."

"*All* androids are less capable than you are," Simon said. "You're—you're something I've never seen before."

You're going to be amazing, he didn't say, as they took seats across from each other. *You* are *amazing*.

"No point in telling them now." A flurry of snowflakes caught his eye, bursting into the window's light only to be carried off by the wind. "By the time the Equinox rolls around, there'll be no one to bring."

"You make it sound like I'm dying," David said, the statement almost coming out as a laugh. "I'm just moving to different hardware."

"And dumping the emotional emulators," Simon pointed out, his tone *dangerously* close to disapproval. He glanced at David, but David was staring out the window. The train began to move, the streetlights sending panes of light sliding rhythmically across David's still features.

"There is that," David said, not turning away from the driving snow. "I suppose that a rapid, significant change in behavior may constitute a change in personality. Such as it is."

"I don't see how it couldn't be." Simon pulled his coat tighter around himself. "Don't you . . . I don't know. Don't you *like* being the person you are now?"

"I'll be the same person." David's voice was far too nonchalant for this conversation. "I'll just act a little differently."

"Because you won't *feel* anything!" Simon's voice was louder than he'd meant it to be. "You won't want things or care about things or be happy about things! You're going to give that up, for what? A faster processor?"

"I will *be* the same *person*," David repeated. "My motivations will remain the same. The emotional emulators are how I relate my thoughts into human-parseable form. They aren't who I am."

"That makes no sense. How can anyone *be* separate from what they want? What makes them happy?"

David turned away from the snow then. "I'm not a *human*, Simon."

"No, but . . ."

"You don't think there's more to me than the expression on my face when I speak to you?"

"Of course there's more!" Simon almost reached for him, but he didn't think he could bear it if David pulled away. "But everything we've done—our friends, our trips, hell, *the sex*—none of it affected you? At all?"

"I'll do some testing," David said, looking back out the window. His hands stayed buried in his pockets. "Disable the emulators from time to time, see how the trajectory of the main logical path changes when they aren't operating."

Simon bit his lip. If he could give David even a *doubt* . . . that had to count for something, didn't it? Agreeing to think about it was a chance. Maybe the only one Simon was going to get.

And staring at the QR code on his ticket, he started to form a plan.

The next few weeks passed in a very carefully cultivated silence.

It wasn't that they were avoiding each other. On the contrary, David was practically glued to Simon's hip, and Simon did absolutely nothing to discourage him. David even came to *bed* with him, and all that that implied—though he tended to slip out to the living room after Simon fell asleep.

And it wasn't that they didn't talk. Far from it. They talked about chores and the news and the programs David watched and the drama going on at Simon's work. They talked all the time: full, rich conversations that formed a perfect ring around the silence at their center.

It couldn't last.

"You got mail," Simon said, coming in from the box and stamping snow off his shoes. David was sitting at the kitchen table, doing a thousand-piece puzzle. He took the envelope from Simon's outstretched hand, and Simon tried his hardest not to grin.

"Who's mailing me?" David frowned at the stamped address. "Nobody even knows I'm here."

Simon was unreasonably pleased to see confusion cross David's features as he inspected the envelope. Ever since Solstice, David had been periodically turning off his emotional emulators, leaving his face blank and actions stiff for hours as he "gathered data." Once, it had lasted an entire day.

"It's the Technologic Intelligence Evaluation Committee," Simon said. "They address it to you and not me as, like, good faith or whatever."

"Why . . ." David started, tearing open the seal. His eyes flickered to life as he skimmed the contents of the letter. "It's an evaluation date." He looked up to Simon, his brow furrowed. "You applied for an identity?"

His voice didn't have quite as much enthusiasm as Simon had imagined when he'd pictured this in his head. "Well, yeah."

"Why?"

Simon let out a small breath. He'd hoped this would be self-evident, once it was pointed out. "I didn't know what else to do."

David's brow furrowed. "What to do . . . about what?"

"I had a subroutine that kept respawning," Simon said, aiming for levity and missing by a mile. He cleared his throat and got serious. "I keep thinking about what you said the day we— the day you came home from Erica's. We've got this whole, I don't know, Möbius strip of trust issues. You can't feel safe without proof. And I can hope you're not going to keep testing me, but I *know* that the uncertainty interferes with your programming, and you hate that, so . . ." He gestured at the envelope. The solution that would fix *all* of this. "Proof. You'll know you're safe, your anxiety will go away, and you won't need to dump your emotions."

David set the letter aside. He didn't look at Simon. Instead, he continued removing pieces from the box, placing them deliberately onto the table. "So you applied for this because you think it'll fix the discomfort of my emotional emulators."

"Well . . . yeah," Simon said. "It seemed really obvious, once I thought of it."

David placed a piece between two others, connecting them seamlessly on the first try. "It's *very* obvious. I thought of it as soon as I learned it was possible."

Simon frowned, trying to see what he'd missed. "Then . . . why didn't you ask me to put in the application? Why didn't *you* put one in?"

"What happens when I fail?" David said, not taking his eyes off the cardboard pieces.

Simon resisted the urge to reach for his hand. "You won't."

"I'm not a *human*, Simon," David said, looking up finally to meet Simon's gaze. "I can fake it. I can fake it well. I can dim my eyes and change my voice and make all the right movements, but I'm *not* the same as you. I've told you that." He sighed. "All an evaluation can do is prove it."

"I think there's more to you than you give yourself credit for," Simon said.

"And I, having written and implemented every byte of what constitutes *myself*, disagree." There was an edge to David's voice that Simon didn't like. "You're impressed by it because *you don't write code*. So I'll ask again. What happens when I fail? What happens when you have the analysis in your hand and you know for certain that there's nothing special to me. That I'm an algorithm, no better than any of the others you walk past every day?"

You are better, Simon thought, but David didn't need reassurances from him. David couldn't hope. He needed data.

"You tell me," Simon said, and this time he did reach out, lacing his fingers through David's. "You fail the evaluation, and you have proof. You're just a computer with a particularly impressive set of facial expressions. You fooled me. And then you're *mine*, to serve at my whim until I get tired of you and turn you off." David's eyes widened, but Simon didn't stop. "Do you feel upset? Frightened? Angry? Or have you just identified a scenario where you *should*?"

David withdrew his hand, reaching into the puzzle box again. "I don't know."

"Yes, you *do*," Simon insisted. "I don't pretend to know *how* you work, but you *do*. On some level, you feel things. You feel them so strongly that you're going to disable the most incredible parts of yourself just to feel safe, and you don't *have* to!"

"I can be incredible in other ways," David muttered. He kept his attention on the table, unerringly snapping piece after piece into place. "Better ways."

"Right, the *infinite iterations*," Simon mimicked. "Maybe I'm just too stupid to understand, but—"

"You're not *stupid*!" David glared up at Simon, eyes flickering, and there was static in his voice when he spoke. "You get frustrated and uncertain and you give up. But what if you didn't *have* to?" Simon kept his eyes on David, not letting them stray to the bookshelf where he still kept his university notebooks, *just in case*. He got the distinct impression that David could see him not looking. "What if you had the choice to accomplish everything you'd ever set out to do? You'd give that up just to *feel*?"

A month ago, Simon would have said *yes*. Now, with his throat burning and his future filled with an empty clawing sensation, he wasn't so sure.

"You're sure you want that?" he asked, instead of answering. The silence between them was cracking, and he needed to be careful where he stepped, or everything would shatter. "There isn't . . . *anything* in that code that you'll miss?"

"Nothing that makes sense." David's voice was edging into a monotone as he tapped the last few pieces into place. "I don't understand. *Your* sensors shut off when their input becomes painful. I have a problem processing the input from *my* code, and I've figured out how to fix it. Why is that such a problem for *you*?"

Because I love you, Simon thought.

"You're leaving," he said instead.

"I'm *changing*," David corrected him. "You'll still be able to contact me, speak to me, even visit me. I can create an avatar and we can speak via video."

"It won't be the same."

"It's good enough for your real family." Simon opened his mouth to protest, but David was barreling on. "And of course, you'll still have this body. Erica can put one of her AIs in it—they'll have the same expressions and sexual coding I do." David pressed in the last piece, right in the center, then finally looked up, meeting Simon's eyes. "I made sure of it. My decision to leave costs you nothing. So, am I free to go?"

The picture that had appeared on the table was of the galaxy, a billion billion stars reaching across the universe, and Simon was suddenly very tired.

David's decision was going to cost him *everything*. And Simon couldn't tell him not to make it. He was going to lose David, one way or another.

"Of course you can go," Simon said, trying to keep the tremor out of his voice. "You've got, what, a week until you switch over?"

"Five days."

They were going to be hell. David was stepping off a ledge, and Simon couldn't bring himself to reach out and pull him back.

"I think . . . maybe I should stay with Erica," David said. "Things are . . . clearer, with her."

Simon's throat tightened, but he couldn't argue. It was David's future. David's choice. Simon *had* to let him make it.

David stared at him a long moment, and then his eyes flickered. "Erica says that's all right with her."

"Good," Simon answered brusquely, and immediately regretted it.

David waited, like he was expecting Simon to say something else. Then, "I'll get my things."

Simon sat at the table, staring at the white speckles of the universe while David packed to leave. He didn't have much, just his clothing and a few trinkets that Andy had bought him. It all fit into one shopping bag, which David slung over his shoulder.

He hesitated when he reached the doorway, his hand on the doorknob.

"I'll send the bike back with the body," he said. "When it's all done."

"Thank you." Simon kept his eyes on the tabletop. He didn't tell David that Erica already knew to keep it. David's experiments had definitely proven *one* conclusion, at least: Simon couldn't bear to see it walking around without David inside. He'd rather dump it down the recycling chute than press a kiss to those empty lips.

It seemed like David was going to say something else, but there was only the sound of the door. It opened and shut, leaving nothing but a freezing draft.

CHAPTER NINETEEN

IT'S COMPLICATED

"**T**his is a bitch move, Rayner," Andy said, pulling on her boots. "This is your *last chance* to see him, and you're staying home. Nice."

"It's more complicated than that," Simon insisted. He was sitting on the couch in yesterday's clothes, waiting for Andy to leave so he could hit the liquor.

"I think you're *making* it more complicated than that," Andy said. Simon didn't answer, just sat there and tried not to shiver when her departure let in an icy wind.

The door slammed, and he stared at it resentfully.

He wasn't *making* it complicated. It *was* complicated.

Simon collapsed onto the couch and stared at the ceiling.

It was his own fault. Against all his better judgment, he'd fallen in love with an android. Was it such a surprise that the android wanted to be . . . well, a *better* android? It probably beat being a pining, lovestruck idiot any day.

It wasn't David's fault that Simon wanted *him* to be a lovestruck idiot too. Telling him the truth would just snarl everything up further—turn David's decision into a question of what *Simon* wanted—and that wouldn't help anything.

Better to let him go. Wish him well after it was done.

Not that David would care, at that point.

Simon tuned in to a stream, some dumb sci-fi holo appearing across his view of the ceiling. He tried to pay attention, to take the focus off the speculation of what part of the process was probably happening now. What the process even was.

He should've gone to work, found some task to keep his mind off everything. Hell, he should go *now*—he should get off the couch and put some clean clothes on and call a car and go do something productive. *Anything.*

He batted that plan around for the better part of an hour, always distracted by thoughts of whether David was done yet, and what it felt like to suddenly be in a new body *that wasn't even a body*. At least it couldn't hurt him, not like last time, not without the sensor lace. Not in a way Simon understood, anyway.

But then again, Simon had *never* really understood David.

It hadn't mattered so far.

Simon rolled off the couch, the last five days of misgivings hitting him all at once. Five days of staring at the icon of David's face, wanting to call and knowing he couldn't.

Whatever he is, I love him, and I can't let him do this alone.

Whatever it felt like to move into that big, empty, blind space, Simon couldn't make it better. But he could make sure David knew there was someone there who loved him. Loved him even when he couldn't understand. Loved him even when his heart was breaking.

Trying to wrestle his jacket on, Simon stumbled and hit the side of the table, hard. It was probably going to leave a bruise, but that was Tomorrow Simon's problem. Right now, he needed to get his boots on, needed to call a car, needed to get to Erica's friend's—*where even was that?*—he needed to text Andy—

He opened the door and took half a step outside before hitting what felt like a brick wall.

David had been standing there, hand raised like he was deciding whether to knock, and Simon, not expecting anyone, had barreled straight into him. David hadn't budged a fraction of an inch, leaving Simon recoiling and almost tripping over his feet.

"What are you—"

"I thought I should—"

"I couldn't—"

They both paused.

"What are you doing here?" Simon finally asked. "I thought today was your big day."

"I've missed you." David fidgeted with the buttons of a coat Simon didn't recognize. "More than I thought I would. The whole time we were setting up the sync, I was thinking . . . It's stupid, but I wished you were there to hold my hand." He reached out, lacing his fingers between Simon's. "And I was thinking about what a stupid, inconsequential action it was to take someone's hand. But the knowledge that I would never do it again . . ." He looked up at Simon. "I couldn't turn it off. Loneliness is an utterly negative emotion, and I couldn't turn it off."

"I'm sorry. I should have been there in the first place." Simon tried to focus on his words and not be distracted by the giddy heartbreak of seeing David one last time. "I'm gonna tell you something, and it's not because I'm trying to change your mind. It's because you deserve to know." David opened his mouth, and Simon barreled on before he could chicken out *again.* "I love you. And I didn't want to tell you because I didn't want you to feel pressured to stay, but you know what? Fuck it. I'm going to love you even if you leave. Because, don't get me wrong: I love going places with you. I love watching you learn how stuff works and playing soccer even when Andy beats both of us *together,* and I love—"

"The sex," David supplied, an obliging smile playing at his lips, and Simon nodded vigorously.

"I *love* the sex, it's *so* good. But I don't need it. I would love you even if I could never touch you again. Because I love your sense of humor and the questions you ask and the way you make me *think* about things. I love the person I am when I'm with you, and if that's all I get, then *that* is what I will love about you. If I have to love you by texting a mainframe, then *that is how I will love you.*"

And that was that, then. The ball was in David's court, and whatever he did with it, Simon would be there to support him. Whatever he needed.

Simon felt like he should be panting, like the crushing grip on his heart should be blocking his air as he waited.

"You could . . . love me," David said, feeling out the words, "even if I could never feel love in return?"

The thought made the bottom drop out of Simon's stomach, but he nodded. "If deleting that code is what you need to do—what you need to *be* . . . to be happy? Then do it." He reached out, taking David's hand. "I thought it would be best to stay home today, that it would be too hard to watch you become something so different, but I was wrong. Because it's not about *me*, it's about you. If you say you'll still be the same, in all the ways that matter, then I should believe you. And if you want to change, then I should be there to support you."

"Oh," David said. He held Simon's hand between both of his own, his thumb stroking thoughtfully over the skin. "Oh."

"'Oh'?" Simon had . . . kind of expected more than that. Sure, David didn't have the greatest grasp on social norms, but usually it was a bad sign to say *I love you* and get back *Oh*.

"That is a lovely sentiment," David said slowly.

"But?" Simon asked, and oh shit, he was getting *broken up with*—

"But love is not a new data point."

Simon gaped. "You *knew* I loved you? Does *everyone* around here see right through me?"

"You aren't subtle." David's chuckle turned sober. "But I knew the idea of the evaluation would occur to you eventually, and I . . . *feared* what would happen when I failed. What it would feel like when you stopped." A week ago, David would have delivered this in a monotone. Now, his words were dull with resignation. "So I decided I would rather feel nothing. Direct my efforts toward what I knew I *could* achieve."

"So then . . . what changed?"

"Everything," David said. Then he grinned wide. "Because nothing."

"I don't follow."

David gestured broadly. "The evaluation still looms. And I still believe I'll fail. I believe I can put everything I have into trying and still be unable to prove that what I feel is real." He took Simon's hands, squeezing tight. "And without *any solid data whatsoever*, I came to the same conclusion you did. I believe you'll love me anyway."

"I will." Simon kissed his knuckles. "Even if I can't—"

"No, you're not understanding. I turned down a *certainty*, based on a *belief*. It's irrational and annoying, and I don't want it to change." David beamed, a brilliance that had nothing to do with his LEDs. "You make me *hopeful*. I think that's worth being irrational for."

Simon hugged him. Right there in the freezing doorway, with snow blowing in around their legs, he put everything he felt into that one, simple gesture. David hugged him back, his arms resting around Simon's waist.

"I meant what I said," Simon mumbled against David's shoulder. "I will love you in any way I get to. But I am *fucking* glad to hear that."

"I couldn't turn down the chance of an Equinox cookout with your mother," David said, and Simon snorted.

"We've gotta take you to a beach."

"See some more of Andy's shows."

"And the *sex*," Simon said.

"*So* much sex," David agreed, turning toward Simon for a kiss.

It lasted until he ran out of air, and then some.

CHAPTER TWENTY

HAPPILY EVER AFTER

"**T**his is supposed to be *spring*," Simon grumbled, looking around the train station accusingly. His friends ignored him. "Everything is dead. We haven't passed one living green thing since we left the house."

"Don't exaggerate," David said. He was in a way better mood than Simon, probably because he didn't have to feel the unfair, unreasonable cold.

"Point to one green thing, right now," Simon challenged him. Wordlessly, David held up his tray of cupcakes. He'd been indoctrinated into Andy's "every important event needs a baked good" school of thought, and she'd helped him decorate them with icing grass and little chocolate eggs.

Simon had stolen four of them during the decoration process. They were delicious.

"That's not what I meant, and you know it," he grouched, pulling up his sleeve to let the ticket kiosk scan his wrist. Beside him, Andy and David did the same.

It was fifteen minutes before the train arrived, letting Simon get just cold enough to really appreciate the heat inside the car.

Andy pulled David down next to her, and Simon sat across from him, the same way he had on the way home from Solstice. Simon had made that return trip thinking it would be the last one they'd ever take together. He'd stared out the window and watched the snowflakes swirl through the blackness.

Now, he could see David's face reflected in the glass, appearing to float over the landscape outside. The landscape which, Simon had to admit, *was* starting to turn green under the bright morning sun.

"Almost warm enough for Everest, eh," Andy said, nudging David in the ribs.

"Not until mid-May," David said. "Sure you don't want to come?"

"I'll stay where there's air," Simon said.

Andy nodded. "No offense, but some of Earth's great marvels you're going to have to see by yourself."

The trip went by fast, and all too soon they were standing at the edge of the park, watching the rented car drive away. Behind them, the Rayner clan's Equinox gathering was in full swing.

"You sure you want to do this?" Andy asked. Simon nodded, taking the tray of cupcakes. With his other hand he reached out, lacing his fingers through David's.

"You really don't *have* to tell them about me," David offered, but Simon shook his head. He'd made that mistake once. He wasn't going to make it again. Someone called his name, but Simon ignored it. Instead, he leaned in, pressing a quick kiss to David's lips.

"Of course I'm going to tell them. You're my favorite story."

Dear Reader,

Thank you for reading Hazel Domain's *Freethinker*!

We know your time is precious and you have many, many entertainment options, so it means a lot that you've chosen to spend your time reading. We really hope you enjoyed it.

We'd be honored if you'd consider posting a review—good or bad—on sites like **Amazon, Barnes & Noble, Kobo, Goodreads, Twitter, Facebook, Tumblr,** and your blog or website. We'd also be honored if you told your friends and family about this book. Word of mouth is a book's lifeblood!

For more information on upcoming releases, author interviews, blog tours, contests, giveaways, and more, please sign up for our weekly, spam-free newsletter and visit us around the web:

Newsletter: riptidepublishing.com/newsletter
Twitter: twitter.com/RiptideBooks
Facebook: facebook.com/RiptidePublishing
Goodreads: tinyurl.com/RiptideOnGoodreads
Tumblr: riptidepublishing.tumblr.com

Thank you so much for Reading the Rainbow!

RiptidePublishing.com

ALSO BY
HAZEL DOMAIN

The Powers That Be series
Any Price
Any Cost
Broken Contracts

ABOUT
THE AUTHOR

Hazel Domain is a cryptid who escaped Ohio and can now be found roaming the woods of eastern Maine. Hazel spends their time fixing computers, fiddling with databases, making renaissance faire costumes and, when all alternatives have been exhausted, writing.

Hazel has five Nanowrimo certificates, a doctorate in parapsychology, and a cat.

Tumblr: tumblr.com/hazeldomain
Twitter: twitter.com/HazelDomain
TikTok: tiktok.com/@theehazeldomain

Enjoy more stories like
Freethinker
at RiptidePublishing.com!

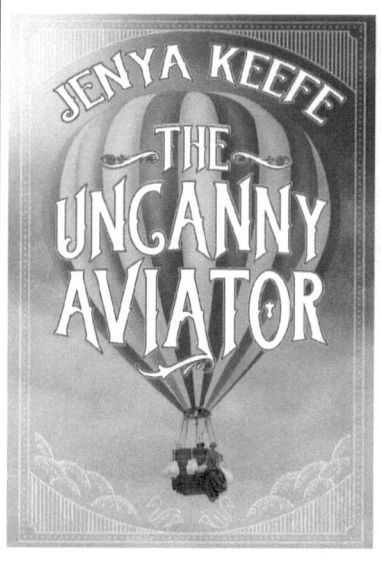